JOINING UP

by
John Jack McGuire

CHAPTER ONE

The wagon driver shouted out a resounding "Whoa," as he pulled the freighter to a clattering stop. He grinned widely as the agile young soldier hopped over a cargo crate to land softly on the sidewalk. The man continued to watch in undisguised admiration as Captain Andrew Whelan an officer in Brooklyn's famous Fourteenth regiment strode smartly up the street. Yes, Andrew was resplendent this brisk spring day not only wearing his dress blue tunic, but those red pantaloons used by his regiment in battle. No one could possibly mistake the nature of his mission.

Those were his thoughts as he strode the cobblestone walkway leading to Saint John's Home. He looked up and grimaced at the tall, foreboding, red brick walls made even more ominous by shards of glass embedded atop its boundaries.

Joining Up

Andrew approached the black iron gates guarding the entrance and pulled on the bell cord. Moments later a gray haired old codger poked his head from the doorway and said "If the Army's out after any of our lads the Union's in a heap of trouble." Andrew chuckled and removed a slip of paper from his pocket. "No, I'm here to see a Mister Gingrich I believe he's the headmaster."

"Yes, he is that, you'll find him in that building across the yard. His office is just above that doorway."

Andrew tipped his cap to the man and proceeded across the compound.

A sudden breeze snapped at his cheeks forcing him to grab the brim of his hat. Here it was late March and he felt chilled, not so much by the weather as the foreboding fortress like walls. The whole caged in atmosphere left him ill at ease. His apprehension most likely tempered by the knowledge someone close to him lingered in such a place.

These were his reflections as he pushed through the doorway and entered the building. A dark hallway led to a narrow staircase. The plank steps groaned in response to each upward step.

A final creak announced his arrival at the next landing. Andrew scrunched up his eyes to become accustomed to the dimly lit interior. He walked toward the door marked Headmaster and let the brass knocker fall against the striker plate. There was no reply so after a minute he swung the knocker again, but with a bit more effort. "I hope this is something of great importance," shouted the loud angry voice from the other side. The door swung open and a short, chubby, bespectacled person in his late forties stood in the doorway shaking in anger. Andrew had to suppress a cough to conceal his amusement at the man's antics. *"I'm sorry to have disturbed you, but I'm trying to locate Mister*

Gingrich, the Headmaster."

"Oh, yes, err, I'm Gingrich, how can I help you?"

"My name is Andrew Whelan I'm with the Fourteenth Regiment. My brother Will was placed with your orphanage several months ago. I wanted to see how he's getting on." The request seemed to startle the Headmaster. He looked anxiously toward a nearby closet and said *"This is quite the coincidence I was just talking to Will and another*

3

boy about some missing food." Gingrich
walked hurriedly to the closet and
opened the door. Two teenagers, with
heads bowed, eyes fixed on the floor
stepped into the room. They appeared
cowered like frightened puppies in
some sort of jeopardy. The taller
boy finally raised his eyes. The next
instant he beamed with excitement.
"Andrew, Andrew, is that really you,"
he shouted bounding across the room
to embrace the uniformed Captain. The
brothers hugged and pushed at each other
in the rough house style siblings often
do. They continued a full two minutes
before realizing others were present.
Andrew finally stepped back and held
his brother at arm's length. He looked
over at the Headmaster and said "Well
Mister Gingrich, what has Will and
the other lad done to warrant a visit
to the Headmaster's office?" Gingrich
hesitated, almost gasping for words.
He licked his lips while searching his
lungs for air. Finally, he opened his
mouth and wheezed "They stole food
from the kitchen they needed to be
disciplined for that." Andrew looked
over at the other boy and noticed an
object hanging across his back. He
walked over removed it from the lad's

shoulders and dangled it in the air. Andrew held it for a moment measuring its weight before snapping it loudly on the floor. "Now there's a cat of nine tails you could tan a man's hide with. You wouldn't use that on children would you Mister Gingrich?"

"It wasn't the first time these two stole food. They needed to be made an example of."

"We took the leftovers Andrew. They would have been fed to the hogs next, isn't that right, Bob?" Will explained. "It was the leftovers just as Will said," Bobby replied. "We were hungry and it was headed for the garbage heap" Will explained. "That's no excuse," Gingrich whined. "They broke the rules and they had to be punished".

"Can't argue with a word like that. Use punishment myself when it's necessary.´ Never flogged a man though breaks the spirit I'm told," Andrew responded

"Corporal punishment is an effective tool I use it liberally," Gingrich sniveled. "Do you now, did you ever feel a piece of rawhide on your own rump?"

"I was educated in private school we had no disciplinary problems."

"There's a twist I'd like to discuss, but not now.

You never been hit a lick yourself yet you enjoy laying leather on another man," Andrew replied, his voice booming now with emotion. "Well, let me tell you something about my Brother Will. He lost his Mother and Father in a God awful fire. Lost everything he ever had including his home. Can you tell me why he's being prodded over a plate of beans?"

"Your brother was placed here by the State because he and his friend were caught wandering the streets. They were sleeping in a livery stable. I've been trying to get them to uphold the laws of this institution and it hasn't been easy," Gingrich wailed.

"Well, if it wasn't for the war I'd be relieving you of any trouble they're causing, but I'm on a short leave and I wanted to visit with my brother. Do you have any laws against that?"

"Oh, no, not at all, it's not visiting day, but we'll make exceptions for the army," the Headmaster said with relieved resignation. He placed an old top hat on his head and left the room.

Minutes later Andrew was pacing the boys sleeping quarters, a dormitory like room devoid of furniture. Will and Bobby watched the tall captain exhaust his anger with every stride; at times covering the full length of the room with only a few steps. Finally, Will broke the silence, "If we could join the regiment you wouldn't have to fret so much." Andrew stopped in mid stride looked directly into his little brothers face and said, "I'd sooner see you getting your hide tanned than have you ducking grape shot."

"But Johnny Flynn and Abner McCoy left here a week ago to become drummer boys with the Sixty ninth Didn't they Bob?" Will replied. Bobby nodded his head in agreement. "Look, at least you're getting some schooling here and you'll need to do a whole lot of growing before you can tuck your feet in army boots," Andrew countered. "And Besides, Major Jordan promised me he would get you transferred to the Delehanty Boarding School right here in Brooklyn." Will looked over at his sidekick who he realized was upset by this current turn of events. He knew Bobby valued loyalty above anything. Over these past few months their friendship became stronger because of the hardships they shared. Will looked

back at his older brother and asked
"How's about Bobby, we been sort of
watching out for each other."

"I can understand you asking for
your friend, but the best I can do
is ask Major Jordan if he can work
it out, that okay by you boys?" Bobby
stood up and said "That'll be fine by
me I'm obliged to you for trying."
Will, looked hard at his friend for a
moment realizing how awkward this was
for him. He moved next to his sidekick
placed a hand on his shoulder and said
"We made it this far, Bob, we'll sort
it out no matter what happens." Andrew
grinned at his younger brother's grit.
He reached into his tunic slipped out
a small brown bag and poured the contents over the bed. "I suppose you
lads don't want any of this licorice
candy." The captain reached over and
selected a strip for himself before the
stunned boys realized what was being
offered. An instant later they dove
onto the bed and began devouring the
sweet tasting treats.

Andrew watched as the youngsters
became children again. Toying and
yanking at the strips of licorice like
boys do the world over. Rassling one
moment and boxing with each other the

next. He couldn't help noticing how different they were. Bobby was quick and darting like a sprinter while Will was loose and deliberate, resembling a long distance runner. Will was nearly six inches taller, a lean slender version of himself with that dark brown tightly curled hair piled high on his head, Andrew thought. Bobby on the other hand had straight jet black hair that hung loosely down his neck. This, together with his dark brown friendly eyes gave him an almost Indian like appearance.

While Will had deep sad blue eyes made more ridiculous by his constant smile. Direct opposites mused the captain, mentally comparing the lad's obvious attributes.

As the boys frolicked Andrew noticed the shadows creeping through the room's one small window. He walked over to Will placed his hand on his shoulder and said "I've got a train to catch little brother, but before I leave I want you both to promise you'll behave until I arrange for a transfer." As if in unison the boys shouted a resounding "Yes." They walked Andrew to the front gate and watched until he faded from view.

At that moment they planned their escape. The thought of spending even a few months more in Saint John's spurred them into activity. Not that they were treated consistently bad.

Actually, most of the teaching priests were good mannered and fair. It was Gingrich, the sallow faced Headmaster who should have been a prison guard that prompted their actions.

Seeing Andrew in uniform also influenced their decision. They yearned to join the Fourteenth Regiment and wear that red boarded blue kepi hat. The boys dreamed of donning that blue tunic, the red pants and white leggings that set the Brooklyn Regiment aside from other units.

The following Sunday the boys awoke early and watched their roommates file out for Sunday Mass. Afterwards the entire student body; the teachers and staff would assemble for the traditional Sabbath breakfast. Nobody in the home misses the one meal where you can have eggs, sausage, ham, pancakes, bacon and globs of it. The kids at Saint John's lived for Sunday breakfast; except today if your name happened to be Will Whelan or Bobby Ambrose. Their stomachs ached from the smell of all those goodies. They stuffed a small linen sack with stale bread and rotten fruit saved from other meals.

The aroma of all that food signaled their departure. Will led the way out of the dorm to a nearby staircase.

He bounded up the steps with his friend closely behind. The sound of creaking wood was barely audible, but to their ears it was louder than drum beats. Each muffled noise raised their attention level and announced to the world their impending escape. After arriving at the top step a wooden door blocked their exit. Will pressed his palms on the door but, to his surprise it opened with a large bang. The sound echoed through the compound causing the lads to lay face down on the roof top. A dog barked nearby causing a howl from other hounds. Surely, this canine chorus would give them away. Bobby peered over the side and noticed a priest in the compound below shading his eyes and looking up. He beckoned Will to stay low.

It seemed like hours, but minutes later he peered over again and the clergyman had disappeared. They worked their way to the point where the building meets the outside wall.

Each had stuffed their pockets with old socks for this eventuality. The protruding glass atop those walls appeared even more menacing from up close. "I'll go first," Will whispered and without hesitation pulled him self up onto the wall. Bobby laughed nervously, knowing his friend is totally without fear. He watched his sidekick adopt a low silhouette to pick his way through the protruding glass. Reaching a nearby tree Will jumped and disappeared in the branches. The smaller Bobby had to jump to reach the wall, but his athletic ability allowed him to do just as his sidekick. He made his way through the menacing objects and leaped into the tree. Minutes later the boys greeted each other with handshakes outside the confines of the Home.

The taller Will immediately left the boundaries of the tree and walked swiftly across the open meadow. Again, Bobby laughed, but this time almost hysterically at his partner's boundless courage. While everyone was gorging themselves at breakfast they were skedaddling to freedom.

Bobby followed his companion at a safe distance. He watched him turn out onto a wide thoroughfare and only then rushed to his side. "We did it Will, doggone it, we did it." Will looked at his friend and laughed louder than he had in months. "Yep, we sure did, but I won't feel safe till were on that ferryboat." Bobby needed to almost run to keep up with his friend's longer gait. Will walked around people out onto the street and back onto the sidewalk. He was trying to blend in with the throng. As usual the streets of Brooklyn were clogged with freight wagons of every description. Teamsters maneuvered their horse or mule drawn carts expertly through these narrow thoroughfare's. Everything seemed to be funneling down to the harbor. The boys willingly joined this sea of humanity and caravan of merchants.

Will reached into a cart to snatch a bunch of bananas.

"Here, try one of these," he said, tossing Bobby a piece of the yellow fruit. "Be careful Will or the cops are gonna be on us for sure."

"Not if we eat em real quick," Will insisted as he stuffed the remaining bunch under his shirt. Bobby once more had to chuckle as his sidekick finished his second not so ripe banana.

Taking a cue from his partner he peeled the fruit and ate it quickly. A moment later Will reached into another cart and began running with some merchandise. Bobby followed him into a narrow alley. Will sat down and held up a bucket of strawberries. "You know Will you act like you been doing this before, like it's natural to you, but we can't just take everything we see, it's stealing."

"No, it's foraging, Andrew said in the Army they go out and forage for food when they're hungry so we're foraging," Will replied. "But we're not in the Army and if they catch us we'll go back to the home real quick," said Bobby.

"Well, we won't go back hungry" Will said, and stuffed a fistful of strawberries into his mouth. Bobby shrugged his shoulders and plopped down next to his sidekick. Seconds later they were alternating the berries with an occasional banana.

Having satisfied their hunger they proceeded toward the harbor. Great wooden piers reached out into the water. Vessels were being loaded and unloaded on either side. Longshoremen and Dock workers moved equipment in a constant orderly stream. Flags of all the nations of the world flew high above the decks of these anchored freighters.

Products from every State in the Union found their way to this port. Some adventurers even slip their wares through the blockaded South. It was all mingled together on Brooklyn's docks; along with soldiers and sailors in strange uniforms. The boys moved amongst this hustle and bustle trying to blend into the mix.

Their immediate task was to locate the New Jersey Ferry Boat. Chances of them being returned to the home would be slim once they crossed the river. They walked swiftly, but carefully following the crowd. Will led the way with that long gait of his. He'd nod to his companion or point in a certain direction and off they'd go. The two inseparable friends maneuvered through the tangled multitude as one.

Bobby noticed a mounted policeman surveying the passerby's searching the sea of faces. He noticed Will move abreast of a Union Soldier as if accompanying him.

Suddenly the copper prodded the animal forward into the crowd. People scattered as the proud animal nosed through the throng. Bobby moved closer to his chum as the mounted officer raised his baton and pointed into the assemblage, seemingly at Will. "I've got you now, stop where ye are," The cop shouted. Bobby clenched his fists in anticipation just as a bedraggled foreign sailor bolted from the assemblage and ran towards a nearby wharf. With hoof beats clattering the mounted officer galloped after him. A sigh of relief and then laughter rose from the crowd when the trapped seaman jumped into the water.

It seemed the harbor was alive with soldiers and sailors.

The color of most Union uniforms was blue, but there were a variety of shades ranging from butternut too gray. All this was especially troubling to young Bobby. He turned to Will after noticing one conscript dressed in a grayish blue and said "I swear Will you'd reckon the Army would know enough to dress a fella in the same color. How else is a man to tell a Yankee from a Reb?" Will nodded his head in agreement. "Andrew said some of them Southern boys don't have any uniform at all they just pick up their muskets and join in."

"Wish we coulda had it that easy. Shucks, we'd have been fighting them by now and chasing them cross the fields all the way to Dixie," Bobby lamented.

Will approached a lanky Corporal who was leaning against a light pole smoking a pipe. As the man puffed away the smoke curled in their faces. "Can I help ye lads?" the man said in a thick Irish brogue. "Do you know where the ferry is?" Will asked.

"Is it the Jersey Ferry or the Staten Island Ferry ye'll be wanting?"

"We're going to Jersey City," Will replied.

"It's just a wee bit farther, downtown," the Corporal responded pointing his pipe towards the street.

"Thanks sir, we're obliged," shouted Bobby.

"Right O, me bucko, Right o', the soldier snapped back.

Will, who loves to mimic said "The Corporal is surely from Dublin a fine Irish lad."

Their pace quickened buoyed by the knowledge they were getting closer to their goal. They walked for another half hour before Will spotted the ferry house, a beautiful wooden planked building with shiny brass decorations.

Bobby grabbed his sidekicks arm holding it firmly for a moment before saying "I swear Will; you act like you done this all before. You know what I mean, like it's a walk in the park." Will looked intently as his schoolmate realizing he was posing a serious question. "It ain't that way at all," he said. "I'm just doing what's natural. I just don't think about it too much is all."

"Well, I just want you to know I'm proud to follow your lead," Bobby replied self consciously.

A loud blast from a ships horn announced the arrival of the ferry boat. It banged against the dock with timbers shrieking their opposition. The sounds of whistles mixed with blasts of steam of steel slamming against steel added to the din. They watched in fascination as people scurried off both sides of this wonderful ship. "There's room for a thousand passengers on that ship," Bobby shouted. The sounds of freight wagons of horse's hooves thumping on wooden planks assaulted their eardrums. Teamsters snapped their whips cursing and snarling at their beasts urging them forward. A mounted policeman on a huge black horse with wild crazy eyes directed the embarking traffic onto *the broad avenue. The horse wheels and moves sideways its hooves stomping the cobblestones. Suddenly it rears, its long legs pawing at the air. The beautiful animal spins, pirouettes in mid air, its proud rider putting on a show for the crowd.*

The boys are pushed forward into the ferry house by the surge of the crowd. Will reaches into his pocket and yanks out a small leather purse. Bobby looks at him and shouts "The sign says ten cents have we got enough?" Will nods yes. "Sure do, we saved eighty five cents this year."

"I hope it lasts till we find the Regiment," Bobby sighed.

Will carefully counted out their fare before wrapping the remaining coins in the pouch and stuffing it in his pants. The crowd separates into two lines, but continues to squeeze towards the entrance. The surge continues pressing every one forward into narrow lanes lined with brass pipe. Two uniformed ticket takers work feverishly to accommodate this mass of humanity while three armed policemen peer intently into the crowd.

Finally, they're forced into a single lane to pay their fare. Bobby tries to avoid directly looking at the man when he plops the coins into his hands. He's relieved when the clerk slides him a ticket stub without incident. Looking back at Will he almost shouts for joy when his companion clears the line. "Doggone it Bob" Will whispered, "We did it, we'll be safe once we get to Jersey City."

With a collective sigh they strolled up the gangplank and boarded the ship. The lads walked to the stern then bounded up a short stairway to the promenade deck. In youthful exuberance the boys celebrate their momentary victory. "I swear Will, there's clipper ships out there just as sweet as you please," Bobby shouted. "And look, there's a Navy Frigate I wonder where they're headed," he continued.

"Out to sea I reckon" Will answered, amused by his friend's exuberance. A clipper ship moved slowly into a nearby dock with sailors throwing large hawsers to dockworkers who loop them around piers. Smaller vessels prowled the harbor in every direction, coursing the river like water bugs in a stream.

Other people crowd on board to stroll the decks. Some walk aimlessly, but young couples on Sunday dates exchange

glances with their lovers. A group of
musicians strum guitars while humming
an unfamiliar tune. An older Negro man
sits alone plucking a banjo. The inviting music causes the boys to sit down
and tap their feet to the melody.

The cargo deck was almost full of
every conceivable type of wagon both
Military and Civilian. The last to board
as the gates clanged behind him was
Dinky Dolan's three wagons. Dinky was
a Sutler for the Tenth Massachusett's.
He is traveling to Philadelphia to load
up with fresh goods he could sell to
the Regiment. Daniel drove the wagon
directly behind Dolan. He is a short,
well-muscled Negro boy of fifteen.
Timothy drove the last wagon. He is
a tall, extremely thin Negro boy of
eighteen. A glance at Timothy would
lead a person to think the lad was
downright sickly. Dinky himself is a
short, slight, red headed Irishman of
fifty years. His beard and the rest of
any hair he has left on his head was a
matted gray. He is never without his
dark blue derby hat or matching coat.
His white shirt is a soiled brown from
the tobacco he chewed incessantly. The
chaw moved from side to side, his jaw
swelling depending on its location.

Dolan's cheeks showed the faint color of crimson otherwise his skin is a ghostly white.

Looking at him with that face full of stubble a person would think the man needed a shave. Considering his clothing and entire personal being one could easily conclude he was in dire need of a good soap and water scrubbing.

Timothy's wagon wheels were flush against the rear gate. He stumbled forward as the boat pulled away from the dock. Dinky was cutting off a bit of tobacco as Timothy approached. He pushed a piece in his mouth and offered a hunk to Timothy. "Lordie, no, oh Lordie no, the sky's a falling," Timothy groaned. Daniel took Dinky's offering and quickly worked it around his jaw. "Jest like honey Mister Dink," Daniel exclaimed. But Timothy was turning a pale green between the ship heaving and the smell of tobacco. He crawled back to his wagon and scrambled underneath to lie on the deck. Dinky grabbed Daniel by the arm and said "Watch the wagons, I'll be walking about." Daniel nodded yes as Dinky proceeded on his way.

The boat forged ahead in a rough sea with the waves crashing over the cargo deck. Water ran the length of the vessel splashing Timothy and forcing him to the rear of the wagon. Another wave causes him to lose his balance. He fell backward over the gate onto the metal ramp. The vessel lurches again, but Timothy cannot regain his balance on the slippery surface. He grabbed onto a stanchion and shouted "Help me Daniel." Hearing the cries for assistance Daniel jumped from his wagon and hurried to the stern where he spots Timothy hanging off the edge. Once again the ship lurches, but this time swinging Timothy out into the ocean. He Bobs to the surface for a moment before the surging tides yanked him under. Daniel looked around for help, but realizes he's alone. No one has even witnessed his friend being torn from the ship. The waves raise the ship in and out of the water. Daniel's forlorn face etches the hopelessness of the situation. Backing away he raised his hands to the skies in exasperation.

"Ay's real sorry Timothy Ay knows you feared the water. And sure enough it done swallowed you up." Daniel stumbled back to his wagon stunned by the course of events. He weeps in his hands, his body shaking with grief. Again, he looks around, but realizes the hopeless of the situation.

On the passenger deck Dinky propped his body against a brass pole for balance against the ship's rolling. He noticed a uniformed Policeman wearing a gray bowler hat. The Copper alternates fingering his long mustache with swinging a wooden baton. Dinky also notices Will and Bobby and their reactions to the Cop. To Dinky's amusement the boys are definitely avoiding the lawman. He watched as the lads moved close to a woman and two young girls as though they're together. Dinky doesn't see Daniel approach and is startled when the boy taps him on the shoulder. "Timothy done fell overboard," Daniel wailed. "Timothy done what" shouted the outraged Dinky. "The water jest a swallowed him up Mister Dink. He was bobbing there once and swoosh he was done gone."

"Ain't that just fine, the dumb Nigrah gets himself drowned when I need him most. It's me luck, that's what it is, me bloody Irish luck."

"What kinda luck yanked Timothy into the water is what ay's wants to know." Daniel responded.

"Ye better get back to the wagons or they'll be saying a prayer over more than one Darky this day."

"Yes sir Mister Dink," Daniel moaned as he drifted away.

Dinky's eyes searched the deck as he contemplates his situation. A Burly Stevedore catches his attention for a moment, but his gaze continually returns to the runaways. He spots a well-dressed man gives him some thought, but even more intently now his focus falls on Will and Bobby.

Satisfied with his choice he ambles over to the boys and sits down. He looked directly at Bobby and asked "Have ye ever driven a wagon, Lad?" Bobby peered back at the seedy looking Irishman and politely replied "No, sir." Dinky turned to Will "How about yeself lad, have ye ever set on a buckboard and wished ye could drive a team of horses?"

"I sure did wish I could that's for sure," Will responded.

"Well, me bucko if that's a fact I've got just the job for ye."

"Sorry sir, Bobby and I are headed south to join the army."

"The Army is it, well, if those ain't the finest words my ears ever

*did hear, but you're running in luck
cause I'm with the Army meself."*

"How come you're not wearing a uniform?" Bobby asked. Dinky looked around
before answering. He noticed the Cop
moving closer as though focusing on
the runaways. "I'm' a Sutler Laddy
with the Tenth Massachusetts no need
for a merchant like meself to be wearing a fancy blue coat." The lawman
began edging even closer. Dinky could
see the boys were getting touchy as if
ready to run. He pointed to the Copper
and said "Now if it's fancy ye want
feast ye eyes on this Policeman. He's
a mean Mick I hear. Bashing runaways
with that club is his game." The lawman removed a paper from his wallet.
He looked at the paper and then peered
quizzically at the teenagers. All this
activity heightens their alarm. The
wily Irishman is prompting the situation even further. "If ye worked for
Dinky Dolan there ain't a Copper in
the world who'd fuss with ye. Sure and
ye'll be hauling gear for good ol Abe
Lincoln."

"I reckon there's something to what
he's saying," Will remarked. "But I
sure did want to wear Union Blue,"
Bobby chimed in. Hearing that, Dinky

reached into his coat and yanked out an Army cap. With a flourish he placed it squarely on the lads head.

"We'll be swearing you in down the road a piece," shouted Dolan. "Least ways we'll be headed down South," Bobby agreed. "Let's do it then," Will responded.

The boys shook hands with the mule-skinner who flashed his crooked snaggle toothed grin. "Ah, ye won't be sorry ye joined up with Dinky Dolan lads, but we best be getting below. We'll be rolling off this scow before ye can say Killarney," shouted Dinky. He looked over at the Cop and tipped his cap to him as they passed by. The lawman returned the gesture and walked merrily on his way.

Dinky led the boys to a gangway and down the stairs to his wagons. Daniel's face widened into a knowing grin as they approached; darned if that sly old Dolan didn't talk a couple of white boys into joining up with his wagon train. "Daniel," Dinky shouted, "I want ye to show Will and Bobby here how to drive a wagon. Larn em good now cause they'll be moving down the road with us." The grizzled Irishman spat out a stream of tobacco juice and whacked the lead mule's rump with his open hand before returning to the front wagon.

Daniel guided the runaways to the rear wagon. The boys touched the leather straps and harnesses that secured the mules together. They pushed against the huge wagon wheels as if testing their balance. Bobby is more concerned with the animals. He tried to pat one on its back, but removed his hand quickly when the mule quivered. "These critters don't look too friendly to me," Bobby observed. "Y'all ain't gotta fret none about them, they just foller right along. Feed and water them every day and they's real happy," Daniel drawled. "But how do we make them stop and go," Will asked. The agile Black Boy hopped up on the wagon followed quickly by the runaways. Daniel picked up the reins and held them loosely in his hands. "Yank on this one here and they go right. Yank on this other one and they go left. Holler whoa and pull back like this and they stops." Daniel demonstrated each action separately. "Y'all ain't gonna have to fuss much 'cause these critters been a following along like this since they was foaled," he added. Bobby was just a bit hesitant as he watched the Negro lad's skill-ful exhibition. "You sure do make it look easy, Daniel, but I don't think it is. I hear mules can get doggone stubborn," he reasoned. "Y'all don't have to fret none with these animals, they's as tame as a hound dog."

A blast of the ships whistle signaled they were nearing the dock. Teamsters began limbering up their whips as their animals strained against their bind-ings. Dinky wound his way between the wagons to join the group. He motioned Will to come down from the buckboard. The lanky teenager quickly jumped to the ground. "Have ye ever ridden a horse?" Dolan asked. "My uncle used to let me ride his old plow horse," Will replied. "Is that a fact," said the Irishman, well, come along laddy ye'll be a riding Martha." Dinky took Will by the hand and led him to the first wagon. A second later he was being hoisted onto the lead Mule. "I ain't sure I can do this Mister Dolan." But Dinky wasn't one to bear any of the lad's anxious protests. He was the type who threw a body in the water if nec-essary. Just set there on old Martha and she'll take you and that wagon off of this barge."

Joining Up

It was too late to argue with the muleskinner the Ferry whistle drowned out every other noise. There was the sound of steel on steel mixed with the thumping of heavy timbers as the ship settled into its berth. No time now for worry or alarm. The gates banged open allowing the line of freighters to disembark.

The front wagons moved down the ramp to the cobblestone streets. Minutes later the entire line pressed forward. Dinky Clicked to his mules to start them in motion. "Hold her steady lad ye'll be a muleskinner afore ye know it," he shouted to Will his shrill voice mixing with a host of other sounds. All the while young Will is bouncing along holding on tightly to Martha's harness. His thoughts are to survive this bevy of moving hooves and stomping feet. To remain seated on this ungainly equine animal no matter what. Bobby is of a similar mind, but his eyes are fixed on his lead animal. Go straight he pleads silently to the critters. He grips the reins tightly unwilling to allow his mule team to move even slightly off course. It is an hour before either boy becomes comfortable with their assigned tasks. By this time they have cleared the busy thoroughfare and proceeding in a long caravan of vehicles into a setting sun.

A scant few miles later Dinky eased his wagon into a wide meadow and pulled it to a stop. Will quickly jumped to the ground to rush back to his side-kick. "How'd it go, Bob? Did you have any trouble with the mules?" Bobby exhaled for a moment before relaxing his grip on the reins. "God knows it was about as scary as I can get, but I'm doggoned glad we got to do it."

Dinky walked up followed by Daniel who always remained a respectful dis-tance behind the grizzled Irishman. "Ye've done a man's work this day me buckoes it's time we rested the stock." Will sidled up to Bobby's lead mule to pat him on the rump. The critter quickly rewarded him with a kick in the shins. Dinky rushed over and sank his crooked teeth into the animal's ear. The critter whined in pain before the muleskinner released his hold. "That's how ye larn a mule not to kick. Now ye and yer sidekick can go and fetch wood for the fire."

The runaways rushed across the meadow frolicking cheerfully as they went. This for sure was a moment they dreamed of; being free from the walls of that dreadful home.

The runaways ran full out to a nearby wooded area shouting in celebration of their triumph. They had waited for this moment and wanted to revel in it. Gathering wood on their own was a chore they really enjoyed.

Returning to camp arms full of kindling Will voiced his concern over their present situation. I don't know what to think about this Dinky Dolan fellow." Bobby shook his head in agreement. "Can't really say what he is, Will. He's this a way and that, sort of peculiar in a way."

Will, couldn't help laugh at his partner's observation. "Sure ain't the ordinary sort," he replied. "Smells something awful," Bobby said holding his fingers on his nose. "That's for sure his name should have been stinky stead of Dinky." Will agreed.

The muleskinner had already started a fire. There was a pot sitting in the embers simmering away. Daniel removed the traces from the animals and tethered them under a group of trees. The boys piled their wood next to the blaze to watch Dolan fuss with the cooking. "Sit down lads; in a wee bit ye'll be feasting on the foinest Mulligan stew this side of Killarney." Daniel sauntered over and handed Dinky a large linen sack. The Irishman grabbed it and dumped a load of eating utensils on a blanket. "Here ye be lads a gift from dear old Dinky Dolan the finest Sutler in Abe Lincoln's army. Ain't that a fact, Daniel?" The colored boy nodded his head in agreement. He gave a set of utensils to the runaways. Dinky pulled the ladle from the pot and tasted it. "Ah, ye've done it again Mister Dolan, ye've done it again, he said."

The boys can not help laughing at the irascible Irishman.

They watched him dip the ladle again before withdrawing it heaping full of stew. Daniel offered his plate and Dinky filled it to the brim, but the aroma of the food is too much for boys just out of a home where chow was scarce. Unable to disguise their hunger any further they rushed forward. The obliging muleskinner began scooping food into their tin platters. With stomachs aching they plopped down on their haunches and spooned the hot stew into waiting gullets. On this occasion with bellies aching for sustenance the two normally well-mannered youngsters ignored all sense of propriety. They ate like wild puppies finally given their turn at the carcass.

Dinky watched in amusement as his new drivers devoured his slum gullion. He pulled another pot from the fire, bounced some hot rolls in his hands before flipping a few to Daniel and the boys. The Irishman reached for his ever present jug and took a long swig. "I swear Will can you believe it hot rolls shouted the elated Bobby. "Nope, but we'll be a mighty long time remembering this day," Will replied.

At nightfall Daniel produced a jug of water and filled the runaway's cups. The boys were finishing their second helping silhouetted by the campfire. Dinky was busily searching through his wares scattering unwanted items as he looked. He located a wooden cup that he placed on a blanket.

Ceremoniously now he opened a shiny wooden box and placed it alongside the cup. Next he withdrew a slim dagger from the box and held it up to the sky. The runaways were finished their feasting and lying comfortably on their backs. Dolan rose to his feet with the knife sitting in the palms of both hands. The camfire light flickered across his face

and he grinned wickedly. Moving closer
to the lads he stared down at them and
asked "Are ye ready to sign the Dolan
papers?" The stuffed teenagers were so
full of food they can hardly move. Will
braced himself on an elbow looked at
Dolan and moaned "What kind of papers
are you talking about?" The muleskinner cut two hunks of tobacco from his
plug and handed one to each boy. "If
yer gonna be muleskinners ye have to
learn to chew tobacco." Bobby took the
weed like substance and queried "Do
we have too." Dinky grinned exposing
his broken teeth "It's the only way
me buckoes." First Will and then his
sidekick bit into the brown substance.
Daniel helped himself to a large chunk
and worked it around his jaw with obvious relish. The boys watched the Black
teenager and attempted to do likewise.
"This stuff got a kinda strong taste,"
Will observed.

Dinky meanwhile was into his ritual.
He raised the weapon high in the air
mumbling some unintelligible words as
if making an offering to the Gods. He
held the knife in one hand and pressed
it into his wrist. A spurt of blood ran
down his arm. He picked up the cup and
allowed the claret to drip freely into

the bowl. "Are ye ready to add a bit of ye blood to mine to make this official," shouted the Irishman. "Can't we do it tomorrow," groaned Bobby gagging on the Tobacco. "I hope yer not afraid of nipping ye fingers and drawing a bit of blood," growled Dinky. "Me, no," said Bobby "I'm just a wondering is all, ain't you Will." But his friend was having problems of his own. He's feeling woozy and wondering how to rid his mouth of the poisonous weed. "This ain't no time to be wondering Bob we best do as he says and be done with it quick as we can," Will groaned. "Yep, I reckon we do let me have that knife" Bobby replied thoroughly accepting his partner's advice. He wobbled to his feet stumbled over to the blanket and grabbed the knife. Without hesitation he nicked his finger allowing the blood mix with the muleskinners. Will, who is also green in the gills sick, joined his friend at the blanket where the whole world appeared to be spinning. Wiping his eyes trying to clear his vision Will took the knife and added his blood to the bowl. Dinky grabbed the cup dipped a quill into it and stirred it all together. Taking

a piece of parchment he dipped the
pen into the bowl and with a flourish
signed his name. Bobby grabbed the pen
and quickly added his signature Will
slipped to the ground and spit out the
remaining tobacco juice before adding
his name to the paper. "Ye've mixed
yer blood with mine lads if ye break
ye word the Dolan curse will follow
ye until the buzzards are chewing at
ye bones," Dinky bellowed. "Shuck's
all we did was sign our names." Will
reasoned.

"Ay laddie that ye did. Ye signed on
till Harpers Ferry or ye soul will burn
in hell. Ye'll feel the Goblins at ye
necks if ye do me wrong." Dolan's eyes
became fiery red. He laughed loudly
his face twisting into a broken toothed
grin. The flickering fire roared for
an instant to another devilish Dolan
shriek. He continued to bound about the
campsite. "It's done me laddy's it's
done. We'll see what kind of cloth yer
cut from," The Irishman screeched.

Dinky continued his ritual dancing
about the fire, kicking his feet high
in the air. Minutes later the frisky
muleskinner seemed to tire. He reached
for his flask took· a huge swallow and

sat down by the fire. Dolan shrugged his shoulders and removed his bowler hat from his head before slumping heavily on the blanket. "Paddy McGinty an Irishman of note fell into a fortune and bought himself a goat," he repeated it over and over in slurred speech.

Daniel led the boys to the wagons. Earlier he placed a piece of canvas between two of the carts to fashion a tent. The brown skinned boy pulled blankets from under the buckboard for each of them. Will and his partner were quick to lie down. "We been wondering Daniel are you and Dinky friends?" Bobby asked. "Dinky's about as crazy as a coot, he signed me up in blood jest like he done to y'all, but the man don't treat me all that bad and he feeds me real good. He's bout all the family I got," Daniel responded.

"How'd you like being friends with us," Will queried.

"Shucks, White boys don't have Colored folks as they friends," drawled the Black teenager. "Seems like we can change all that," Bobby responded. "I just hope's we ain't gonna do it in blood," Daniel joked. Sick as they were the runaways had to laugh at Daniel's remark. Will held out his hand and said

"No, but we could shake hands on it."
The three teenagers laughed loudly and
clasped hands in a joint salute to
friendship.

CHAPTER TWO

The gallant Fourteenth forget them
not, our gallant boys who, for nations
life, have stood amid the battle grime
and noise, baptized in its flames and
blood! The brave Fourteenth, how well
they wrought for freedom, let our annals
tell, a cheer for those who stoutly
fought, a tear for those who nobly
fell. Those words, spoken by William
Burleigh at a recruiting rally in 1862
have been placed on a plaque that First
Sergeant Terry Gormley of Company E is
about to hang in Andrew's headquarters
tent. The Sergeant enlisted the aid
of a Brooklyn lady to fashion the Red
White and Blue cloth. He attached it
to a pole alongside the entrance flap
so it will receive its deserved attention. He stepped back to view his handiwork just as Captain Whelan brushed
his way into the canvas shelter. The
tall Andrew removed his hat that had

become crooked when he ducked to enter the tent. "The top of the morning to you Sir," The soldier snapped as the officer settled into his camp stool. "Good morning Sergeant I could smell that coffee from the creek," Andrew remarked. Terry filled his company commander's cup and placed it on his writing desk. The Army thrived on the coffee bean and Captain Whelan was no different. He sipped the dark brew for a moment enjoying its flavor before noticing the Poem fluttering from the post. "As long as there's a Fourteenth Regiment those words we'll be remembered Sergeant Gormley." The thankful soldier self consciously adjusted his tunic trying to hide his emotion. Terry was a patriot above anything else; a man deeply proud of his Regiment.

A courier rushed into the tent and placed a packet on the table. "A message from Regimental Headquarters," said the messenger. He clicked his boots together snapped off a salute and left. Andrew opened the leather case removed a document and read it quickly. "Form the Company Sergeant Gormley we're moving out." With that he handed his subordinate the dispatch. "Ah yes, I see we'll be taking a wee march," he observed, reading the orders. "Eight days rations and all the extra rounds a man can carry. Looks like our lads will be in for a good scrap afore this is over," the heavy set Top Sergeant commented. He squared up his shoulders pushed his chin out in practiced military fashion before stepping out of the tent. Gormley marched down the company street where he encountered Corporal's Duffy and Schoenfield sitting under a lean to. "We'll be moving out at noon form the company at the edge of the meadow. Have the lads draw eight day's rations and all the extra cartridges they can carry," shouted the top kick. The men responded without a word. They ran to the neat rows of tents shouting orders. Suddenly, the lazy camp where soldiers lounged in their tents sipping coffee erupted into frenzied activity. Troopers looked to their muskets first carefully checking cartridge boxes and cap pouches before filling canteens. Rations were evenly placed in haversacks to distribute the weight.

Flashes of Red and Blue dominated the field as the men prepared their gear. The battle tested veterans carefully donned their red vested brass buttoned jackets before falling into the line of March. Their red legged trousers gave them the appearance of French light Infantry. This was not a parade uniform, but no matter how frayed or sullied, this was the combat clothing they couldn't and refused to fight without. The Brooklyn militiamen formed into two columns awaiting further orders.

They moved out at noon heading in what the men determined to be the general direction of Fredericksburg. A place many of these same troopers had their baptism under fire. Andrew led the company with Sergeant Gormley close behind. Corporal Duffy brought up the left rear column while Corporal Schoefield kept the right side from straggling. At dusk the march was halted within a mile of the Rappahannock.

During such large movements of the army a man can only see what is to his front or immediate flanks. Their focus is on the few hundred yards of dirt they'll be fighting in. Knowing those limitations Andrew roused his company at eleven P. M. and slowly advanced toward the river. Their mission was to assist the engineers in moving the pontoons into position. Thanks to a

thick fog they completed this assign-
ment without incident. Knowing the coming daylight would lift the haze the
Captain deployed his red legged devils
along the riverbank as skirmishers.

The bridge builders were in the
water connecting their pontoons when
the mist slowly dissolved. Observing
this the Rebels began a steady musket
fire from rifle pits on the opposite
bank. "Give it right back to them,"
Andrew shouted.

His volunteers responded instantly
firing a volley into the enemy's positions. A battery of secesh artillery
put the entire Union effort under direct
bombardment. Shells were exploding with
deadly accuracy amongst the engineers
on the river and Andrew's supporting
Infantry. Confederate sharpshooters
were pouring a deadly hail of lead into
the attacking Federal's. The men of
the Fourteenth fired back furiously,
but had to withdraw when their ammunition was expended. Sergeant Gormley
picked an expended mini ball from his
forearm as they pulled back. Eight of
his lads were wounded and three brave
souls would never see the sunset.

The pontoon corps incurred even
harsher casualties. More than half of

their compliment lay dead or wounded.
Time after time they carried their
boats to the waters edge, but were
forced to take cover from the raking
hail of lead.

A messenger crawled through the
brush with mini balls clicking at the
branches. "Colonel Fowler is asking
for volunteers to get those pontoons
across" The young soldier shouted.
Andrew looked at Sergeant Gormley who
was tying a strip of cloth around his
wound. "Have the men stack arms, we'll
be helping the engineers get that
bridge across," he said confidently.
The dispatch carrier grinned at the
Captain's self assured attitude. He
snapped off a quick salute before hur-
rying off with the reply. Andrew stood
up and began walking amongst the men.
His top kick adopted the same pose
in deliberate defiance of the cracking
bullets.

"Hold up on the firing lad's. We'll
be stacking those muskets for a wee
bit. The Engineers will sure need our
help," Gormley explained. "Are we
volunteering or is this your doing"
shouted a voice from the ranks followed by the nervous laughter of men
resigned to their fate.

With arms stacked the men seemed to adopt an air of collective boldness. "C'mon lad's we'll be pushing those boats to the other side," urged the First Sergeant. With a loud yell the soldiers headed for the wagons bearing the boats. Once more screaming their defiance the red legged troopers took hold of the freighters and rushed them towards the river. The Rebel fire pits bellowed with smoke and a volley of singing mini balls struck men and wagon alike, halting their charge. In this exposed position the men flattened against the freighters looking for cover. Andrew realized their position was untenable in face of such heavy musket fire. They were inside the enemy's killing zone. Going back would be just as dangerous. He sprang to his feet with lead nipping at his cap and spattering against the wagons. "Forward men let's get them boats across so we can put some steel on those Johnnies in the pits," Captain Whelan shouted. The response was immediate. The men pushed their wagons forward and with a loud roar dropped the pontoons into the water. Enemy bullets tore into the troopers wounding many and ripping chunks of wood from the boats, but a cheer echoed from the Union ranks confirming the pontoons were launched.

Men of the twenty fourth Michigan and the Sixth Wisconsin held in reserve for this moment rushed for the shore and plunged into the boats. Dozens were felled by intense Rebel musketry. At this point Union artillery took the Confederate rifle pits under bombardment. The Federal infantry on the banks joined in with heavy rifle fire. This brief respite allowed the men in the boats to grab oars and pull towards the other shore. In the furious excitement men of the Fourteenth without arms joined the other regiments in the assault. Andrew ordered First Sergeant Gormley to muster the remaining men and return to their original position.

Corporal's Duffy and Schofield along with six privates were caught up with the enthusiasm of the attack. They picked up oars and amidst a hail of bullets paddled to the other side. Once across, men from the various Regiments jumped into waist deep water to scramble up the banks.

The Secessionists' appeared stunned by the bold nature of the assault. Groups of Gray clad Rebels bolted their positions in extreme disorder. Some scattered through the woods at the sight of two screaming Red legged Corporals wielding paddles. The victorious Union maneuver accounted for more than one hundred and twenty Rebel prisoners.

Andrew's unit suffered eleven wounded three dead and one missing. Private Jason Kick a former roustabout from the Brooklyn Docks was last seen scrambling up the river bank towards the enemy rifle pits swinging a broken oar. While he is listed as missing in action the men privately hope he was captured. "Those Reb's will be a needing a doggoned battalion of men just to guard old Jason," Sergeant Gormley mused. "He's a mean one alright. Our lads don't know whether to feel sorry for the Secesh or be thanking the lord for their own providence," laughed the top kick.

CHAPTER THREE

Dinky's three wagons proceeded through the New Jersey countryside amid a long procession of freighters. Bobby drove the Muleskinner's rear wagon with Will perched on the buckboard next to him. Dinky guided the lead wagon with Daniel plum in the middle. The boys were more relaxed now that leading a team of mules is an everyday occurrence. They click their tongues at the mules to move them along; and snap the whip at the lead critters ear to get her attention. Habits they've picked up just from watching Dolan or his Black teenage cohort. They're wearing pieces of cloth over their faces to protect against the oppressive dust. It becomes imbedded in both skin and clothes. They've learned to spit out streams of water they swilled to clear grit from caked lips. The boys look much like any other teamster pushing a cart along these clogged roads.

What captivated the runaways most was the Army wagons carrying supplies towards the battlefields of the South. "Do you reckon we'll ever get close enough to see some real fighting?" Bobby asked. "Don't know why not" Will replied. "All's we gotta do is just find the Regiment. I'm guessing if there's any action they'll be near it," he added. "Doggoned if I ain't aching to pull on a pair of those Red britches," Bobby remarked. "The way I heard the story is they fought one battle in Union Blue and got whipped good. They been wearing Red ever since," Will revealed reaching for the canteen. He took a huge swig and swizzled it around in his mouth for a moment before spewing it out. His partner repeated the gesture, but expertly spit his stream of dust laden water on the hind most mules' rump. "You know I can just close my eyes and see us charging across the field with the Regiment and chasing those rebs back to Dixie," was Bobby's wistful response. "Andrew says those Southern boys are about as tough a soldier as you can find. They can march all night and fight all day," countered

Will knowing his friend would react to such a statement. Sure enough, Bobby propped himself up on his haunches eyes flashing with intensity. "That may be so, but no man has a right to own another man and that's why they're fighting this war and that's why the Union's gotta win." Will grinned at his friend's reply knowing how fervent he was about fairness towards others. A matter they discussed often and were in total agreement.

Suddenly they were off the road under a group of trees. Because of their chatter the runaways didn't notice their team follow Daniel's directly off the path. They did see a large contingent of Union soldiers setting up bivouac in a nearby meadow. Dinky appeared very excited as he tethered his wagon to a large sapling. "If ye want to eat ye best tend the animals," he shouted. By this time the lads were accustomed to the Irishman's antics. Even though this was a bit early in the day to set up camp they abided his wishes. Actually, it was the friendly Black boy who helped them most. The patient Daniel showed them through example how to treat animals. He cared for them first making sure they had clean water and excellent browse. At night he'd corral them close to the tents for safety. Throughout these many days of travel the lads watched their Black friend's every move. They learned quickly as boys their age do the world over; absorbing his practiced routine to the fullest. Somewhere down the road in the near future they would earn the title Muleskinner.

With their chores finished the three boys watched Dinky build a roaring fire. He pulled a length of canvas from his wagon that he fashioned as a tent between two trees. The busy Irishman tapped a keg and set it up on a larger barrel. Taking hold of Daniel's arm Will whispered "what's he up to?" The Colored boy chuckled a bit trying not to laugh out loud. "Oh, Good ol Dinky's setting his self up for business. He'll be whipping up a mess of Johnny cakes next." Sure enough, Dolan began mixing flour with water in a large bowl. "What kind of business could he be getting way out here?" Again, Daniel held back a laugh, but pointed to the army encampment across the road. "Y'all see those bluecoats long side the road over there? Ol Dinky's after they pokes." The befuddled Bobby looked at his Black friend for a moment before asking "What's a poke, Daniel?" The Colored boy shook his head in disbelief in a don't that white boy know nothing manner. "That's what you keep's your money in, one of these." Daniel swung a leather pouch in the air. "In about a minute Dinky's gonna lay a slab of bacon on that fire and wait for the honeybee's to gather," the Black boy drawled. "Since when do honeybees like bacon" Bobby inquired. It was Will now shaking his head wondering why his friend was so misinformed. "It's like fishing," Will explained, "only it's the soldiers Dinky's looking to hook." Suddenly Bobby appeared to sense what was going on. "Just the whiff of that bacon would get me," he laughed. "It sure enough got my belly a talking and a rolling," Daniel added.

The three hungry teenagers edged closer to the simmering chow. Dinky was hurriedly ladling pancakes on the grill. He took long strips of bacon and hung them on a wire above the fire. The dripping fat left an aroma wafting across the meadow. Noticing the boys close by he motioned for them to get their mess gear. "C'mon, ye little beggars get ye fill of these vittles

and get yeselves back to the animals.
I don't want ye under me foot," hollered the Irishman. "Yes sir, Mister
Dink," Daniel drawled as he obediently led the boys towards the pungent
grub. Dolan heaped generous helpings
of the food onto their plates as they
passed by. "Now get yeselves out of
me sight," he warned. The youngsters
cradled their plates in their arms and
returned to their lean to.

Once in the shelter the lads settled down to devour their food. "Can't
say Dinky doesn't feed a fellow," Will
remarked. Three nodding heads confirmed his observation.

"Nope," Daniel said "Ol Dinky don't
hold back none on rations the man loves
to eat his self and the Lord knows he
loves his applejack," grinned the Black
boy. "I never did taste pancakes like
this afore," Bobby commented. "They's
Johnny Cakes, the Army boys just load
up on them. What they don't eat today
they puts in their packs and saves for
another day," Daniel informed them.

Three soldiers, A Sergeant, a
Corporal, and a Private meandered
into the camp from across the road;
their noses leading them directly to
Dinky's fire. "The top of the evening

to ye lads and what regiment are ye with," asked Dolan. "The Second New Jersey," replied the tall light haired Sergeant.

"The second is it?" Dinky replied. "A fine outfit I'm told. Could I interest ye lads in a sip of cider," teased the Irishman. "Not if it's sweet cider, I like something a bit stronger. Something that might clear a man's throat," answered the Top kick. Dolan laughed wickedly as he drew a cup of Applejack from the keg. He handed the brew to the man who grabbed it anxiously. The Sergeant took a small sip swilling it around in his mouth for a moment. Obviously satisfied he tilted his head back and drained the cup. "Ahh, now there's a drink a man could get to like," gasped the Topkick struggling to speak from the effects of Dinky's home made firewater. Everyone was grinning now knowing there's food and drink available. "How about those Johnny cakes I sure could eat a stack of those with a hunk of bacon," asked the heavy set well-muscled Corporal. "Yeah, and maybe we could wash it down with some applejack," added the baby faced young private. "Sit yeselves down by the fire lads and I'll fetch ye some of the finest grub ye ever set ye eyes upon," bragged Dolan.

The soldiers made themselves comfortable loosening their jackets before spreading out around the blaze. "How much you get for the chow," asked the Sergeant. Dinky flashed his snaggle toothed grin as the bluebellies were settling into his lair. "Don't ye be worrying about a little money we'll settle that up later," Dolan replied. "Ye do have money," he added, suspiciously. "Can't spend it out here in the country," replied the top kick. The Sergeant jingled a money pouch in his hand. His companions reached into their jackets to show their pokes. "It's little enough a poor ol peddler like meself can do for fighting men like yeselves, little enough indeed," wailed the wily Irishman.

Daniel and the runaways moved in amongst the trees to observe the activities. "See what that old fox went and did he got those rabbits to sashay right into the wood shed," Daniel said, setting down under the large oak. "Those soldiers look big enough to take care of themselves," Bobby insisted. "Bobby knows how to defend himself Daniel he can't reckon how a man Dinky's size can take care of three troopers," Will said, trying to explain his partners reasoning. "For Dinky it's gonna be bout as easy as snipping beans. He's gonna fill them bluebellies full of Applejack afore he whacks them up side the head with his club," The Black boy replied. "I don't know about that, but it seems like grown men ought to know that Dinky's a scalawag out after their money," Bobby contended.

As they spoke the shrewd Dolan was busily distributing his home brew to the soldiers. "Here ye be me buck-oes drink up, Old Abe will have ye out there fighting rebs afore ye ever taste grog like this again," Dinky shouted, refilling their mugs. "We'll be back in it soon enough," replied the Sergeant. "I've heard nary a whisper of the bloody war. Have we beaten the bloody devils, yet," asked the cunning Irishman. "I hear we whipped them good at Reynolds landing up around Fredericksburg," The corporal noted. "That's good to hear, but I'd like to see how ye lads measure up to me own outfit the tenth Massachusetts," taunted Dolan. "And who's gonna do the measuring," the Topkick bellowed. Dinky ambled over to a large barrel of liquor. Resting his hands on the lid he looked directly into the Sergeants face. "Sergeant Tim McGrath lifted this very barrel over his head fifteen times and that's a fact," Dinky challenged. The young Private took hold of the keg testing its weight. "Must be quite a man" said the baby faced soldier. Hearing that, the top kick took hold of the barrel and lifted it off the ground. "Would there be a wager in it," inquired the Sergeant. "I've a five dollar gold piece here. I'd be happy to oblige a New Jersey lad for less if it's a bit to rich for ye," The muleskinner jeered.

The soldiers moved off to the side to discuss the matter.

"It wouldn't be an easy lift for any man," whispered the Private. "That's a full keg Sarge do you reckon you can do it," queried the husky Corporal peering back anxiously at the keg. "I'm betting I can" whispered the top kick.

The soldiers ambled back to the fire. "I'll be taking your wager mister Tenth Massachusetts," hollered the sergeant. "Will ye now" said the wily Dolan. "Then we'll be hoisting a few to ye good fortune" he added. Dinky filled all the cups including his own.

The four men drained their mugs in the flickering candlelight; casting a long shadow in the underbrush Dolan quickly refilled their mugs. Much to his delight they're guzzled down once again. "Are there any rules we don't know about?" queried the Corporal. "Nary a one, all the lad has to do is lift this wee barrel over his head sixteen times and ye win," Replied the Irishman. "Would you mind if I tested the weight myself," asked the heavy set two striper. "Have all the tries ye want lad. It's a worthy bit of lifting if I do say so meself." The drunken Corporal circled the barrel peering at it and trying to maintain his balance. Dinky's moonshine was taking its toll on the bluebellies. Finally, the soldier put his arms around the keg, but seemed to have trouble holding it.

After two attempts he raised it to almost chest level. He staggered and fell still clutching the barrel. "It's time to fill ye other leg" shouted Dinky topping off their jugs. The men guzzled the moonshine down in one gulp. "Out of the way men it's my turn to dance with the lady, the sergeant bellowed. Without hesitation he grasped the keg with two hands to check its weight. Taking a deep breath he lifted the barrel over his head to cheers from his comrades who Dolan was busily feeding moonshine.

The sergeant staggered as the count reaches five, but is determined to continue. At eight he is faltering badly, but pushes through the pain. His cronies help remove his jacket, but the overheated man pulled off his shirt for further relief. As the number hit ten he is struggling to push the keg above his shoulders. The veins in his neck are popping from the strain. His friends shout "Eleven," but the bare chest topkick sank to his knees. The drunken soldiers rushed to their leader's side. He staggered to his feet accompanied by his cronies. Together now they approached the keg and surround it. The Sergeant grips it again raising the unyielding barrel to almost shoulder level but, his feet give out causing him to stumble. His partners hold him for a moment, but the top kick falls prostrate. Like wooden toy soldiers they collapsed together in a heap.

Daniel and the runaways have been observing the proceedings with great interest. Dolan is humming an Irish tune throughout the debacle. The scalawag muleskinner seemed to know where this was headed from the outset.

They watched curiously as Dinky removed a vial from his pocket. He poured the contents into three cups before filling them with Cider. Holding the drinks in both hands he prances over to the soldiers and gives one to each. "T'was a fine effort lads ye did yeselves a great service," Railed the wily Irishman. "That's right Sarge," slobbered the Private. "Not another man in the second New Jersey could have done better. I'm proud to serve with you," he added. "The Second molasses," slurred the Corporal. "I reckon my call would be the whole Union Army." Not to be outdone the Private raised his cup and said "I'll drink to that." The comrades pressed their mugs together and downed them with a flourish. "That's right me buckoes drink up and now ye can have a wee nap," laughed Dolan.

Still humming, the cagy Irishman skipped back to his wagon to observe his handiwork. He grinned devilishly as the bluebellies just slumped to the ground. Grabbing a large wooden mallet Dinky returned to the prostrate soldiers for a closer look. Their deep snoring brought a crooked smile to his lips. Satisfied that they're unconscious he dragged them individually to the fire. With careful aim he whacked each man in the noggin with his club before searching their pockets.

"Ay done told y'all Dinky's gonna be taking they pokes," Daniel drawled from the safety of the thicket. "My God Will he's went and killed those soldiers," Bobby exclaimed.

"No he ain't, he jest tapped them alongside they heads a bit. They gonna have an egg on they heads come morning is all," whispered the Black boy. "Looks like Dinky's done this more than once Bob," offered Will. "That ain't no lie," Daniel agreed. "But we best get the wagons ready cause old Dinky's gonna be sasshaying on out of here," he added.

By this time the wily Dolan removed the soldier's uniforms and stuffed them into his wagon. "Ahh, it's been a pleasure doing business with ye fine lads of the Second New Jersey," Dinky railed.

Sure enough, just as Daniel expected the scalawag Muleskinner had them harness the wagons and make a quick return to the highway. Moving with such haste at night made the lads feel like criminals. It was clear Dinky wanted to distance himself from his former camp. For the first few miles they traveled at a quick trot which in itself was unusual. "It just ain't right Will, the man's a crook we gotta do something," Bobby insisted. "You're right as rain" his partner replied in a calm matter of fact voice. "But we're on the run from the home. We gotta bide our time and do this right. Meantime, we're heading south towards the Regiment. Let's get what we can out of this," he added. "I swear Will; you make it sound so easy I wish I would've thought of that." Bobby let the reins relax in his hands. Maybe everything will work out after all he thought.

CHAPTER FOUR

Much like fighters in a large ring the two armies sparred consistently prob- ing for weaknesses.

General Robert E. Lee's Army of Northern Virginia until recently held most of the advantages. Fighting Joe Hookers Army of the Potomac moved reg- ularly shooting left jabs and feint- ing with its right. The First Corps under General Reynolds of which the Fourteenth was attached settled into line on the road leading to Ely's Ford on the Rapidan. It was butternuts against bluebellies, battling it out in the fields near Chancellorsville. This was a slugfest in a one horse town History will long remember.

Company E of the Red Legged Fourteenth was bivouacked in a large field. Andrew sat under a stretched canvas sipping coffee from his canteen cup. His troopers were spread out along three rows of tents with muskets stacked nearby.

Most of the men were writing letters. Others are tending their gear while some just lounge around one of the many campfires brewing their own coffee. Sergeant Gormley sat on a nearby stump cleaning his musket. "A bit of rest doesn't seem to be hurting the men Sergeant," Andrew mused. "No, but the lads will be busting for a brawl afore long. All that marching gets a man's dander up," the top kick responded. "I don't suppose they'll leave us setting here long," the Captain was quick to add. "And you know the boys would crawl to Richmond and back for Fighting Joe Hooker," Terry replied.

Hidden amongst the thickly wooded forest a Brigade of Confederate soldiers from the 5th Alabama prepared to attack.

A Mounted Rebel Captain guided his horse carefully through the tangled scrub pine. No one could have anticipated man or beast moving through such dense undergrowth, but these poorly supplied ill clad Southern Infantrymen had marched through the night to reach this point.

The officer raised his saber and he listened for that unmistakable metal click as his men fix bayonets.

He looked down the line at his unkempt assemblage. A bedraggled legion, some tattered, others hatless and haggard, but at this point in time probably the best infantry in the world. Just as his sword drops a loud familiar rebel yell erupts from his charging followers.

They streamed from the woods firing rapidly at the surprised Federals.

The Union soldiers rushed for their weapons, but many are felled by a volley from the tree line. Andrew gathered a group of troopers to return fire. Sergeant Gormley took careful aim at a charging Rebel who falls before he can shoot. The top kick squeezed off a round striking another running butternut. A group of red legged stragglers scrambled into their position. They deploy immediately, directing their fire into the attacking Southerners. The mounted Rebel Captain entered the clearing and spurred his horse directly at Andrew. The animal is struck in the neck by a musket ball. It stumbled and fell blood gushing from its wound. The enraged Rebel officer swung his saber at

Andrew cutting his uniform. He slashed again slicing Andrew's cheek. Again and again the Rebel Captain slashed, but the retreating Andrew picked up a discarded musket. He parried the blade wielding secessionist forcing the man backwards. Andrew appeared to be gaining an advantage, but when their legs get tangled they fall heavily to the ground. As they're grappling the Southern Gentleman yanked a small pistol from his boot, but Andrew wrestled it away. A rebel soldier wielding a bayonet rushed to help his Officer. Andrews shoots them both.

Two more groups of red legged soldiers from the Fourteenth filter back into the battle. Sergeant Gormley drops a charging secessionist directly in front of their position. Another screeching Butternut is impaled on the top kicks bayonet. Rebel yells dominate the action when another line of secessionists break from the woods. A nearby Union battery decimated their ranks with grape shot.

Another detachment of Red legged troopers pull in. Andrew forms them into a line of skirmishers. The Tall Captain raised his sword to attract another group of arriving soldiers who respond quickly. Andrew directs a volley of musket fire into the attacking enemy. The gray line faltered for a moment. Another volley halts them completely. Captain Whelan raised his Saber in full view of the field just as sergeant Gormley rushed to his side. "We're gonna push them back men" Andrew shouted trying to be heard over the din of battle. "That's a lovely gash ye have on ye cheek Captain Whelan was it ye barber," jibed Gormley. "Set the men up in a skirmish line I want these Rebs pushed back," Andrew ordered his voice booming with intensity. "Wouldn't ye rather run the bloody devils back," queried the Topkick.

"We'll get them moving first then you can have your charge," the Captain replied.

The sergeant moved out amongst the men barking orders as he went. Straight towards their antagonists they walked in a staggered line. They stopped at intervals to fire a volley into the retreating Secessionists. "Step it up lads," Gormley shouted. The red-legged troopers began to trot as the enemy turned back towards the woods. "Smartly, me buckoes, smartly, urged the top kick. Again the Union infantrymen quickened their pace. The rebels were in complete rout when they hit the tree line. "Charge em men, charge," Gormley hollered as he watched the Rebel infantry in full flight. A loud shout rose from the Union lines when the Gray clad soldiers disappeared into the brush.

With dusk settling over the field a solitary musket barked somewhere in the woods. In the distance an artillery flash temporarily brightened the sky. Andrew dipped a rag in a bowl of water. He dabbed it on his face to remove the blood. "That's a beautiful wound Captain Whelan. I believe the Turks call that a decoration of the skin. That is if you're wounded in battle," Gormley stated. "I could have lived quite well without it," Andrew replied. "Did ye see those rebels run when they seen ye bloody face. Like ye were Satan himself," The Topkick laughed. "But we won nothing Sergeant the whole Army gets outflanked and Hooker skedaddled back across the Rapphannock like a rabbit," The fed up Andrew replied. "It's me humble opinion that fighting Joe got his self outfoxed by Robert E. Lee," Gormley declared.

Neither side could call it a decisive victory although the South suffered five thousand less casualties at Chancellor-ville. The North had committed only half its forces during the campaign. Some units never fired their rifles in anger during the battle. Absolutely no advantage was gained by either side.

General Robert E. Lee was given a personal blow during the operation when a bedraggled aide interrupted him while he sipped coffee in his command tent. The man placed a dispatch in his Commanders hand and waited anxiously for a reply. Lee read the note for a moment before gripping his hands to his face. "My God, Jackson is dead I've lost my right arm. It would have been better for the country if the Lord had chosen me in his stead. The victories of the past few days were due to his skill and energy not mine," cried the General. "You're being too harsh on yourself, sir. General Jackson would not have expected you to reproach yourself so," the Aide responded. "President Davis will have to be informed of this terrible loss, but otherwise Chancellorsville has

been a great victory. We can only wonder why our fortune is so tempered" Lee
replied, trying to regain his compo-
sure. "And Stuart's scouts have spotted
Hookers troops moving back across the
Rappahannock at U. S. Ford," stated the
Aide. "Include that in our dispatches
to President Davis he'll be pleased to
know Hookers Army has returned to its
original positions" the shaken General
Lee replied. "Yes Sir," snapped the
Aide. He clicked his boots saluted and
left. The Confederate leader slumped to
his knees and offered a silent prayer
to his fallen friend.

CHAPTER FIVE

In the wake of Chancellorville a sad-
dened President Lincoln stood in the
War Room of the White House reading
dispatches. The gaunt Commander and
Chief visibly disappointed by the news
from the battlefield. One by one he
rolled each scrawled message in a ball
to discard it on the floor. An obviously ill at ease Secretary of War
Edwin Stanton entered the chambers. "I
received your note Mister President,"
murmured the Cabinet member. "Yes, I
wanted you to know I've decided to
relieve Hooker," Honest Abe responded.
"So, it's Burnside's critic who is
next to feel your wrath," Stanton
observed. Pondering his answer the
President ambled over to a map board.
He placed a long scraggly finger on
a red circled portion of the graph.
"It's not wrath Edwin the man had Lee
out gunned here and out manned there

yet he failed to press the advantage. Fully half the Army never fired their rifles at Chancellorsville," Lincoln explained. "The General writes of it as a great victory," offered the Minister. "Yes, strangely he does," agreed the President. "The man bragged to half the Army on what he'd do, but as soon as Lee appeared on his front he lost confidence and assumed defensive positions," continued the Chief Executive. "Who will be his successor?" queried Stanton. "General George Meade will lead the Army of the Potomac. With God's help the Old Engineer will win us a victory or two," said the hopeful emancipator. Secretary of War Stanton left a solitary Commander and Chief to his charts. He knew the tall angular President would spend days examining his maps. The weight of a Nation etched into his countenance while he pondered the fate of the Union.

An unconcerned Dolan meanwhile set up camp in the Philadelphia countryside. He busied himself checking a manifest against a list of commodities. The Sutler wanted a full compliment of supplies for his rendezvous with the Massachusetts Regiment. Daniel and the boys repacked their wagons to Dinky's satisfaction. They lounged under the tent awaiting their next task. "How'd you ever get started working for Dinky Dolan," Will asked the Black boy. "My Mammy and Daddy worked in Mister Dinky's store. Shucks, we jest about lived in that store since I was a pup," Daniel replied. "Didn't you ever go to school?" Bobby inquired.

"Us colored folks don't go to school like you white people does. Ol Dinky had his parson learn me my words and numbers," was the black boy's response. The three friends didn't realize the crafty Irishman was finished with his inventory. With nary a sound Dolan sidled up to the canvas covering to listen to their conversation.

"I didn't reckon a man like Dolan to be a church going person," Will observed. "He sure enough weren't," Daniel drawled. "He and that Parson fellow jest sit around drinking Applejack till they got falling down drunk," the Colored boy added. "Maybe he wasn't a real preacher after all," Bobby remarked. "Ol Crandall Krebs was a Parson all right. My Mammy reckoned the man was evil. A womanizing devil that was done foaled in hell is what she said," howled Daniel. The eavesdropping

Dolan crawled closer, straining to hear every word. "I swear it just ain't right a preacher acting that way. Was he colored?" Bobby asked". "Shucks no, Mister Krebs is just about as white as you is," answered the black boy. Daniel reached around in his pocket for a hunk of tobacco. He offered the boys a chew to which they gagged no in response. The dark skinned youngster worked the wad around in his jaw as the runaways gazed in amazement. "Where's your folks now?" the inquisitive Will asked. "My Daddy went off and got his self all shot up and killed at Second Bull Run," Daniel replied chewing briskly on his wad. "Your Mammy still working in Dinky's store?" asked the Whelan boy curious to find out more about their Black friends childhood. "Mammy just up and left with ol Parson Krebs," Daniel lamented. "You mean she ran away with the Preacher?" was Bobby's open mouthed query. "Said the devil made her do it" drawled the colored boy. "I declare," the compassionate teenage orphan sighed. The Black boy wanted to know something about his companion's predicament. "Y'all gonna fess up to who you running away from," Daniel asked with a knowing grin. "You

gotta swear you won't ever tell anyone else," the tall angular Will queried. "Man, you white people sure are
funny with the swearing and signing
in blood stuff, but I swear if that's
what y'all wants," the friendly Colored
boy laughed. His commentary brought
the spying unscrupulous Muleskinner in
even closer to the boy's shelter. "We
ran away from Saint John's home in
Brooklyn," Will declared. We're gonna
join the Fourteenth regiment soon as
we find out where they are," he added.
"See what I mean about White folks
being funny," the black lad mused.
"About what," Bobby asked. "Shucks, a
colored boy would a stayed in that
home stead a going out and getting
his self shot up." Will walked over
to his friend and lifted his shirt
to expose his scarred back. "Here's
what good old Whip Gingrich gives you
for taking another helping of beans,"
Will exclaimed. Daniel peered at his
new found muleskinners wounds in disbelief. He pressed his hands over the
bruised skin while mouthing an appeal
to the Lord. "Lordy, ay hope's you're
marking this down in your book for
Will here," Daniel prayed. "We'll be
all right long as we don't have to go

back to that home," Will declared. To which the wily Dolan flashed his snaggle toothed grin as he crawled away.

At daybreak the next morning they lined up at the supply depot. A stocky bearded man seemed to be in charge. He shouted orders to his two teenage helpers on the loading dock. Dinky stepped off his wagon to approach the man. "I'll be buying thirty sacks of flour and eight slabs of bacon if that be all right with yeself," Dolan inquired. "Ya, ve got em if you got cash money yust pull up the vagons and ve load em up," answered the stocky bearded man in a heavy German accent. "Move em up" Dinky shouted reaching into his purse for the money. Will took Dolan's lead wagon into the first enclosure while Daniel moved into the one alongside. Bobby nudged his wagon into the remaining stall. "Load em up," shouted the Dutchman to his coworkers. The boys started to haul sacks of flour onto Wills cart when Daniel decided to stretch his legs on the platform. "Those sacks heavy" Will asked the tall blonde headed boy. "Nope" was his curt reply. The other heavy set dark haired boy looked at Daniel and shouted "Get back on your wagon nigger," Bobby

responded immediately, jumping off his
wagon to stand next to his black companion. "You and that nigger better
get back in your wagons," threatened
the dark haired dockworker. "I don't
rightly understand someone doing that
kind of name calling," Bobby declared.
"Ain't nothing to fuss over mister Bob
let's do as he says," Daniel reasoned.
But Will was having none of that sub-
mission nonsense. He moved quickly
over to the platform to stand with his
friends. "Might as well just bop him
partner," he shouted to his sidekick.
"Yeah, c'mon, let's see if a nigger
lover can fight" taunted the heavy
set boy. Bobby jumped from the platform directly in front of his adversary. The young dockworker stuck out
a foot knocking him to the ground,
but the agile runaway jumped to his
feet pumping his left fist into the
husky youth's jaw. Now, the battle was
joined. They circled each other looking for an advantage.

Dinky meanwhile was seeking to
profit from the event. "Are ye going to
let them fight?" Dolan asked. "Und vy
not, Max vont hurt him too much," the
German replied. "I've a bit of a wager
for ye if your lad whips my boy I'll

pay ye double. My lad wins and I owe ye nothing the Irishman proposed. "Ya, that's goot," answered the Dutchman. "Put cash on table und ve got deal" he added. The grinning Dolan bounced his money pouch on the table.

The husky dockworker continued to stalk his faster opponent.

He swung wildly, but Bobby stepped easily out of range landing a left right combination to the jaw. Dinky and the Dutchman got caught up in the excitement of the moment. They moved closer to the action. "Max, mine got, beat him, smash him down mit your fists," urged the German. "I've got news for ye mister provisioner ye boy's getting whipped by a fine broth of a lad, one of me drivers," Dolan shouted in the man's ear. "Vy you not help your brother," the Dutchman hollered at the other dockworker. The tall blonde lad moved menacingly at Bobby. Will smashed his elbow into the boys face knocking him to the ground. "So it's fighting ye want me buckoe well up with ye hands ye blasted kraut, up with ye hands," shouted the Muleskinner slugging the man with a pouch full of coins knocking him flat on his back. Daniel returned to his wagon to watch Bobby land a flurry of punches to Max's midsection dropping him to his knees. Will put the tall blonde boy in a headlock and squeezed the air from his lungs. The bearded Dutchman held the smaller Dolan at arms length fending off his wild swings, but the three instigators had enough. They limped back to their loading docks bruised and beaten. Dinky was quick to press his advantage. "All right lad's let's load up and be on our way," he shouted. Keeping their eyes on their adversaries the four Muleskinners packed their provisions and returned to the highway.

That night they camped in the Philadelphia suburbs. Dolan roasted strips of beef roast he bought from a local farmer. The Muleskinner had been humming Irish tunes all day celebrating their victory. "If it wasn't for me back I'd have whipped that Dutchman good," Dinky exclaimed. "Y'all done a share of scrapping today that's for dang sure," Daniel chimed in. The Irishman slapped the dripping meat between hunks of Amish bread with his hungry drivers waiting in anticipation. "Bobby done all the real fighting," Will declared. He had that boy dizzy as a hoot owl," he added gazing at Dinky's sizzling hot steak dripping gravy on the bread. "Mister Bob got rhythm like I never seen, hands a moving and feet a going like all get out," drawled the Colored boy. "Ah yes, the lad's a natural born prize fighter. If I was back in Dublin we'd make a fortune." Dolan bragged as he slipped the food onto plates. The youngsters leaped for the grub, biting off hunks of bread mixed with red meat and gravy. The Wily Irishman watched the teenagers devour his offering.

CHAPTER SIX

From their encampment in Eastern Virginia Andrew led twenty of his men along a winding stream. The Captain ordered this patrol more to raise the morale of his troopers then military necessity. It was also a relief from the boredom of everyday camp life. Sergeant Gormley walked a few yards in front with the men spread out at similar intervals.

Reaching a wide spot in the brook the top kick signaled for a break. Troopers fanned out in every direction as a precaution against attack. Andrew joined his subordinate who was sitting on a large flat rock. "A bit of biscuit, Sir?" asked the sergeant drawing a tin from his pocket. "None for me thanks I had my share of hard tack this morning," Andrew replied. Gormley laughed and dipped his hard tack in the swift running water. "If ye soak it a bit and drown those wee crawling critters it ain't half bad," joked the top kick.

Corporal Duffy waved from the opposite hill to attract their attention. "A couple of sweet looking Gobblers over there," Duffy remarked pointing to a fenced in area connected to a barn that was itself attached to a smaller shed. "They are lovely" Gormley quipped. "A shame to see them fenced in like bloody convicts" said the trooper. "It is that" the Top kick agreed. "Would ye be against releasing the prisoners" Duffy inquired lighting his pipe. "Not at all lad I'm for rescuing the poor devils," Gormley responded. The corporal waved to Private Henry Cook who immediately ambled over. "We'll be taking those gobblers into custody" Duffy declared. The private turned instantly to the direction of the barn. He nudged two other troopers on the way and they spread out along the fence line. Henry jumped the barrier, but the turkeys scattered. He dived at one and it scooted away.

Andrew crept to the hilltop to watch the operation. "Wouldn't ye know the blighters jest ain't willing to be set loose" mused the sergeant. "There's not much choosing to do. It's our pot or the johnnies," Andrew commented.

By then the birds jumped to the roof of the shed with Henry grasping at their feet. The gobblers leaped to the steeply pitched barn with the private in pursuit. They moved to the ridge pole, but Henry had difficulty negotiating the steep metal covering. Every time he moved close he slipped back. As the struggle continued a large band of Confederate soldiers moved in to investigate. They deployed on the opposite hill overlooking the farm. One of the rebs took careful aim with his rifle and put a bullet close to Henry's feet. "Let go of those birds yank or I'll fill those red britches full of lead," shouted the Johnnie. "Might just give you Rebs a bird if you ask real nice," answered the Union Private. A brisk volley of Minnie balls struck the roof close to the Yankee trooper causing him to lose his balance. He fell to the shed when another burst of fire knocked him to the ground. Private Henry fled for his life running madly back to the tree line.

Andrew's full detail of soldiers assembled at his position. "We'll not be feasting on gobbler today," the captain announced. "We could always fight for them," Corporal Duffy declared. A heavy volley of musket fire crashed into the surrounding branches nipping off twigs.

"Our lads want to scrap over the birds, but I'm thinking the Johnnies have us outflanked and out manned," Gormley observed. Another fusillade of shots crashed into their position from the other side.

"Too much lead coming from that hill looks like we'll be eating hard tack again," Andrew reflected. "Give those butternuts a volley so we can back off this hill," The top sergeant shouted. The troopers responded with a fusillade into the Confederate position. The rebel line opened with smoke as mini balls whizzed through the underbrush.

Andrew's unit began its retreat firing fast as they moved to the next hill. The rebel yell screeched across the field as they watch the union troopers withdraw. A long line of gray clad soldiers moved out of the woods to fire another barrage. "Quick time me buckoes show them blackards the back of ye lovely red britches," sergeant

Gormley bellowed as they moved out of range. No one needed to urge the men any further thought the top kick. They're happy to return safe to their lines this day.

CHAPTER SEVEN

General Robert E. Lee remained convinced his Army of Northern Virginia must take the offensive. To sit near Richmond and await a Federal siege was folly he argued. His plan was to march into Pennsylvania where he could invigorate his army from the resources of the Rich Cumberland Valley. Putting his plan into motion he moved his headquarters north to Culpeper Courthouse.

While General Lee weighed his actions a resplendent General Jeb Stuart entered his office. "You're having a review I hear," Lee queried. "Yes, I thought the men could use a bit of parade before we maneuver into Pennsylvania," Stuart replied. The Commanding General looked at the well dressed Cavalry officer for a moment noticing his brilliantly shined riding boots and sparkling saber. "I gather no women will view this, err, parade,"

Lee asked. "Ah, yes," he replied. "I've been told the ladies of Culpeper will attend," Jeb continued. "The Cumberland Valley should be helpful to our troops" stated the Commanding General. "We'll be eating union beef and the animals will fatten up on Yankee grain," Stuart responded. Lee grew serious. He looked directly into his subordinate's bearded face. "Your cavalry are my eyes and ears Jeb. What I need is for you to stay the right flank and keep me informed" was the Commanding General's passionate plea. "You have my word" the steely eyed cavalryman replied. He saluted his commander and left.

At the Culpeper parade grounds later that afternoon two rows of mounted cavalry were spread nearly a mile across the open field. To their front is an entire division of Texas infantry led by General John B. Hood and his staff of mounted officers.

From off in the distance two riders galloped their horses across the compound. The cavalrymen cheer triumphantly when they recognize the riders as General's Jeb Stuart and Wade Hampton.

A group of women in two separate carriages move up a narrow trail and

stop in front of the mounted officers. Two ladies sporting large sun
bonnets dismount their coach carrying garlands of flowers. Our younger
girls assist the women, holding the
trains of their gowns off the muddy
soil. The ladies draped their flowers
across General's Hampton and Stuart's
mounts bringing cheers from the assembled cavalrymen.

But there's grumbling amongst the
ranks of the bored infantrymen. A tall
grizzled sergeant pointed to the decorated horses and shouted "They ought
a shoot a man for sticking flowers on
his mule," A comment that caused the
remainder of the Texas infantrymen to
jeer derisively at the horse soldiers.
Another foot soldier stepped from the
ranks and hollered "C'mon men, lets go
over and wipe out that whole passel of
mule setters" Again, the men jeered
and hooted their defiance.

Wade Hampton wheeled his mount close
to Stuart's. He reared his horse delib-
erately allowing it to kick its feet
while pawing at the air. "One word and
we'll run those foot slogging beggars
back to Texas," he implored. "Can't
expect men to walk all that way and
have much sense left," Stuart jibed. A

remark both General's laughed at like tickled children.

A murmur from the entire assemblage prompted them to notice another group of riders moving up the path. As they drew closer another murmur rippled through the crowd. One can not mistake the name Lee, Lee, Lee, when it's uttering from a thousand lips.

The field rumbles as the extremely popular Commanding General and staff begin to review the troops. The ladies attempted to adorn Lee's horse Traveler with a bunch of flowers. He politely waved them away bringing a resounding cheer from Hood's Texas infantrymen. "I'm an old infantry commander" General Lee explained to the women. Garlands might be very well for a cavalryman, not I." The Generals aide dismounted and gallantly accepted the bouquet.

Not to be outdone General Lee reared his horse raising another cheer from the captive audience. An instant later he was galloping his mount along the entire length of the first line of cavalrymen. They roared again when he entered the second line of troopers to gallop along their ranks.

The entire assemblage began screaming and shouting their allegiance to Robert E. Lee.

General Stuart saved one more treat for the crowd. He rode to the front of his cavalrymen with his sword raised to tierce point. He paused for a brief moment until he heard the clang of metal as warrior's un-sheathed their sabers. A second later a blood curdling rebel scream announced the charge of a thundering brigade of cavalry. Troopers raced across the field swords glinting in the afternoon sun. The sound of a thousand pounding hooves dominated all else. That is until a battery of artillery laid its barrage on a distant hill. Another battery unleashed its steel on the same target. A fusillade of musket fire roared from a concealed infantry brigade causing smoke to stream across the entire field. No one, but the uninitiated would think this a simulated battle. General Lee appeared captivated by the fury of this mock assault. He turned to his aide and said "I'm afraid if war were not so horrible we would learn to love it."

CHAPTER EIGHT

Dinky's wagons were tethered together in a stockade at the rear of a barn. They have reached an old town named Clinesville on the Eastern bank of the Susequehanna. Small businesses line the main street. Murphy's Saloon displayed a large Beer on Tap sign. Dinky became a friend of Patrick Murphy the bartender and owner. Murphy was a large robust man in his early forties who sported a pot belly.

Will and the boys have since grown tired of tending the stock and guarding the provisions. "Can't reckon why we're not moving on can you Daniel," young Whelan asked. "Mister Dink done found his self a water hole," the black boy replied. "Can't figure where a little man like him puts it all," Bobby wondered. "At least we're eating good" Drawled Daniel munching on a cold sweet potato.

Joining Up

There's a distinctive Dutch Amish
flavor in that section of Pennsylvania.
Farmers wore peculiar wide brimmed
black hats while driving one horse bug-
gies along narrow roads. Bright eyed
pink cheeked women wearing large bonnets tended roadside markets. Polite,
courteous children helped with the
stock or unloaded the big crates of
foodstuffs. There is a variety of fresh
vegetables mixed with slabs of beef
and fresh hams.

Amongst all this abundance there
is concern for the rumblings of War.
Dinky Dolan is not one of those. He's
only out to help his own cause. He
sits at the bar sipping a brew watching Murphy polish beer mugs. "I've
heard the whole Rebel Army is heading north again" said the pot bellied
barkeep. Are they now," the unalarmed
Dolan replied. "Abe's calling for volunteers" Pat declared. "I'd go meself
if it wasn't for me bad back," lied the
Muleskinner. "We're forming a company
to help whip those doggoned secessionists," Murphy said with a burst of
pride. "It's a fine bunch of patriots
ye are to be going off and leaving
all this," Dinky allowed. The bartender held a glass up to the light

closing one eye like a jeweler peering at a precious stone. "I'll not be going meself," grinned the bartender, "I've no one to care for the place," he lamented. "That's too bad Pat you'll be missing a fine scrap," reckoned the wily Dolan. "Councilman Moore will be outside meeting with the lads to help them make up their minds you might say," Murphy explained. "He'll be leading them up the garden path, but he won't do any of the digging," Dinky quipped.

"Ah, I see you know how the tune is played," chuckled the barkeep. I do that" Dolan nodded back.

Groups of men began gathering outside the saloon. A detachment of rag tag militiamen marched a group of civilians through the streets. A horde of young boys followed behind hooting loudly at the potential servicemen. Women peered from windows. Older men looked anxiously at the green recruits.

Councilman Frank Moore entered the saloon and sidled up next to the Muleskinner. "I'll have a sip of ale" Moore said, placing a paper note down on the mahogany. "Ah, it's not an easy task you have at hand this day," Murmured the sympathetic Murphy.

"A man does his duty where he see's
it" the Councilman replied. "It's hard
to reckon those Rebels moving into
Pennsylvania" the Bartender remarked.
"It's that sly old fox Lee. They say
he's trying to pressure Abe

Lincoln into setting down and palavering with those Southern Aristocrats"
said the politician. "You've a bit
of palavering to do yourself," Murphy
interjected. "You're right my friend
let's see how many lads are willing
to fill the breach" he murmured. The
councilman straightened his hat in
the mirror then drained what was left
in the mug. He put on his specs to
read the penciled notes on a parchment. The wary Politician was preparing himself for his flock. Well satisfied he walked slowly out the door.
Murphy hurried after him with Dinky
close behind.

The councilman waved his hands in the
air to assemble the crowd. Like herded
sheep they bunched together awaiting their fate. "All right men tune
it down a bit and we'll get started
here," the Assemblyman shouted. A partially uniformed veteran in the rear
hollered "I reckon you could talk a
rabbit into chasing a fox afore you

get me into falling in line again." A burst of nervous laughter erupted from the gathering. The polished campaigner chuckled himself for a moment waiting for the snickering to simmer out.

"What I'm asking you men for is to protect your womenfolk and children from a bunch of slave herding Rebels. They're pillaging your villages and stealing your crops. Stop them thieving buzzards here in Pennsylvania. Shoulder a musket against the bloody devils invading our land." Councilman Moore stepped back to a loud chorus of cheers. The militiamen set up a table nearby to accept recruits.

Murphy patted the Politician on the shoulder. They watched a line form at the recruitment table. Dinky joined them to observe the proceedings. "A fine choice of words, Councilman if I do say so meself," said the Muleskinner. "That's the truth Frank you've done yourself proud," Murphy chimed in. "A few more nips of ale and I'd have joined up myself," the politician quipped. They broke into laughter until Dinky suddenly spotted Will and Bobby in the line of inductees. He backed into the bar with his new friends unable to keep his eyes off the boys.

The patriotic runaways felt exhilarated by the councilman's speech. "Do you reckon its right for us to join another outfit" asked the concerned Bobby. "You heard the man, there's a need for us here. Besides, Andrew is firm again us joining the army never mind the regiment," was Will's confident reply. "Sure wish Daniel could have come along with us," sighed the dark haired lad. "He reckons Dinky's all the family he got, says he eats good and there's a place for him to sleep every night," replied the tall runaway. "I was thinking about that Dolan curse too. You reckon we ought to worry about that blood oath we took" Bobby asked of his good friend. "I had my fingers crossed all the time.

Curses and devils can't hold on me now," Will insists. "Ah shucks, you should have told me. They'll be coming after me as sure as green apples, I just know it Will," Bobby groaned. "We'll make us up some garlic and onions and cook them under a full moon. You'll have to make a wooden cross and carry it for seventeen days. That'll remove the curse for sure," the Whelan boy said. "You think that will work" asked his friend. "Ain't nothing garlic and onions won't kill" the taller lad said emphatically.

The line kept moving closer as men signed up and were taken off immediately to join the new forming company. When they were only a few feet from the table two men wearing

Pinkerton badges confronted them. "What's your name Son?" The taller light haired man asked. "Its Will Whelan sir," he answered. "And what's your name" he growled at Bobby.

"Bobby Ambrose sir," the shorter boy replied. "Looks like we got em," snapped the other Detective. The men placed the boys between them and led them away. "All's we want to do is join the army" Bobby remarked trying to explain his actions. "It's more likely you'll be wearing leg irons then Union Blue afore this day is out," growled the light haired officer. "Are you allowed to tell us what we done wrong?" Will asked. "Mister Pinkerton doesn't pay us to answer questions," the other detective snapped. Frank Moore walked out of the saloon to join the group. "What's going on here," the Councilman asked. "These boys are wanted in New York, we caught them trying to join the Pennsylvania Militia"

replied the taller Pinkerton. The politician looked squarely at Bobby peering directly into his eyes. "What are
they after you for stealing money or
beating up on old ladies," he sneered.
"We didn't steal nothing or beat up on
nobody," Will answered for his friend.
"I been told you're such bad criminals
they want to send you back in chains,"
Moore responded. "Ain't a thing like
that at all," the Whelan boy insisted.

Dinky strutted out of the saloon humming an Irish tune seemingly unaware of
the situation. Noticing the commotion
he ambled over. "What are ye doing with
me drivers?" he asked. "Do these lads
work for you?" the Politician wanted to
know. "They do that" replied the snaggle
toothed muleskinner. "The Pinkerton's
tell me they're wanted in New York,"
said the sarcastic Politician. "Go on
now, not the very lads I've been risk-
ing life and limb with?" Dolan remarked
in feigned ignorance. "They answer to
the names of the boys they're looking
for," Moore persisted. "Are ye wanted
for some crime," Dinky asked looking
directly at

Will. "Not us mister Dolan" the
Whelan boy answered with his fingers
crossed behind his back. "There you

have it" the muleskinner replied. "Are
ye satisfied?" he added. "No, I'm not,
but we have a law in Pennsylvania that
allows for the boys to be paroled into
the custody of a guardian. Would you
be willing to sign the papers" The
Councilman stated with a suspicious
wink to Dolan. "I would that," Dinky
grinned back. "You'll be taking respon-
sibility for the beggars. If they com-
mit a crime you'll all go to jail"
Moore insisted with a slap of his hand
across the other. "Are ye willing to
do as Councilman Moore says?" Dinky
asked, a question that the grateful
runaways quickly nodded their heads in
approval. "I'll have the papers ready
before you leave. A set of leg irons
will be part of the deal," The politician shouted in a resounding voice.
"Alright lads get yeselves back to the
wagons and be ready to move along,"
Dinky shouted, an order that sounded
more like a reprieve to the frightened
runaways. Their imaginations put them
in leg irons yet here they were running back to Daniel and the wagons.
"I'd be watching those buggers close
if I were you those blackards we'll be
running off," The Councilman shouted
at Dolan. The words were meant more

for the runaways who were scooting off as fast as they could run.

Minutes later in Murphy's saloon Dolan was hosting a celebration. "That was a mighty pretty piece of acting ye did Mister Moore. A wee bit of malarkey" Dolan laughed, downing a growler of beer. "I'm afraid it was those two bloodhounds we should be toasting," Moore railed hoisting a double shot of brandy. "Yer right me buckoe, here's to the Pinkerton's as fine a bunch of fibbers this side of Dublin," the muleskinner shouted. Dinky drew some money out of his pouch and handed it to the Detectives. He took Moore by the arm and slipped him a bit of cash. "Ah, yes, I have those official looking parole papers right here," Moore said handing the documents to Dinky. "It's been a pleasure doing business with such a fine lot of rogues," Dolan laughed. "The drinks are on Dinky Dolan tonight lads I'll be back on the road come morning," the muleskinner shouted.

CHAPTER NINE

Washington D. C. was bustling with activity in recent days. Refugees from the South were camped in every available field surrounding the Capitol. Officials from the North visited the White House daily expressing their concern over Lee's most recent foray into Maryland and Pennsylvania.

The imperturbable President is not one to cry wolf.

He sat at his office desk calmly reading dispatches. Secretary of War Edwin Stanton showed a bit more concern when he entered the room. "Don't look so worried Edwin I've

Got Governors, Mayors and the Lord knows how many other officials advising me to put McClellan back in command of the army," Lincoln murmured. "Everyone thinks you've got the wrong George in charge. For some reason McClellan is the people's favorite General," Stanton replied. Lincoln pushed himself out of the chair to stretch his legs. As of late pacing became something of a habit. "The man's a good soldier and a darn good organizer, but he didn't fight. Hooker now was a good talker who avoided the one fight he could have won. What's the answer Edwin, tell me," Honest Abe asked. "Mister President we must remember with Lee moving his army at will through our towns and valleys and Stuarts Cavalry trying to circle the whole dosh gone Union Army again there's bound to be some err, criticism." The cabinet officer declared. "It's not all bad Edwin I been reading the accounts of the Brandy Station engagement. Our Cavalry under Pleasanton fought Stuart to a stand still. Union Cavalry Edwin there's one for the critics," was the President's animated response. Lincoln rubbed his hands together like someone anticipating a fight. "Yes, our men are finally catching up. The vaunted Rebel Cavalry is meeting Union horse-men every bit their equal," admit-ted the War Minister. The President browsed through a mess of dispatches before locating the one he wanted.

"Here, read this one. We have another hell for leather horseman named Custer. Loves to fight I'm told. We're not in such God awful shape after all," said the enthused Lincoln. "That's all very true Mister President yet the enemy is at this moment at our rear and threatening Pennsylvania. We must not have another Antietam it would be disastrous," stated the Secretary of War. "The army of the Potomac is preparing to confront this invasion. A battle is looming that may well determine the fate of the Union. We can only pray for a great victory," stated the beleaguered Lincoln. He strode to his maps with Secretary Stanton at his side. The two peered at the charts looking at latest Confederate dispositions. Abe drew a line across Pennsylvania with a dark blue crayon. Stanton nodded in agreement.

CHAPTER TEN

Andrew led his bedraggled Company down a dusty wagon road clogged with vehicles. They are headed North in a general movement of the army. They've engaged Lee's invading forces in five skirmishes in as many days. The column moved to the road side as a detachment of Cavalry galloped hurriedly by kicking up more dust. A mule train loaded with cargo slogged forward cutting ruts in the thick clay. Single wagons and coaches move in a seemingly endless stream down the clogged road. "We've had a taste of this road before captain," Sergeant Gormley sputtered clearing the grime from his face.

"This and a few others," agreed the officer. "Where is it do we meet up with the horse soldiers" the Sergeant asked. "According to the maps there's an old barn about five miles up this road we'll rendezvous there," Andrew replied. "It's just a wee stroll in the park," the trooper quipped.

The column approached a plantation that stretched far out into the countryside. A large mansion sat on a knoll overlooking a main house with dozens of smaller cottages nestled between pine trees. A group of Blacks three dozen strong came ambling out of the woods and sat on a rail fence. An older Patriarch type gray haired black man stood at the entrance. "Will Mister Lincoln be coming along this way soon," asked the fatherly colored man. "Ol Abe's back there behind one of those wagon trains. He'll be coming down that trail some time tomorrow," shouted a mud streaked corporal. "Blessed be the Lord, Mister Lincoln is a mighty warrior. Hallelujah, Lord," wailed the old man. "And all the people shall answer and shout amen," murmured a foot slogging infantryman. The Patriarch began humming a tune and started rocking to and fro. His followers joined in with a low chorus of "Halleujah Lord." The old man raised his hands to the heavens and led the group in a song.

Don't you see 'em, comin', comin, comin' Millions from the odder shore?

Glory! Glory Hallelujah! Bless de Lord Forever more!

Don't you see 'em goin', goin' goin'

Past ol' massa's mansion door? Glory! Glory! Halleujah! Bless de Lord forever more! Jordan's stream is runnin' runnin'

Million soldiers passin o'er Lincoln comin' with his chariot Bless de Lord forever more!

"And the Angel of the Lord appeared before him and said you are a man of valor," cried a young private.

The column approached a fork in the road where after checking the maps Andrew signaled his Troopers onto a smaller less traveled plantation road. They marched another two miles in heavy scrub until they reached a clearing. Two dilapidated log cabin type buildings and a barn stood at the opposite end of the field.

"We'll spread out along this tree line," ordered the tall red-legged captain. The troopers began dragging logs to their front to form a barricade. "It's a might quiet for a summer's day not a wee bird in the sky," mused Gormley.

"Those Butternuts must have stolen some coffee I can smell it brewing,"

Andrew noted. He pointed to a puff of smoke rising from a campfire in the vicinity of the buildings. Suddenly there is the roar of artillery. A round of solid shot smashed into the nearest structure tearing it into splinters. Two more shells explode close to the other buildings. "Those artillery lads have dropped a bit of iron on their coffee pot," laughed the Sergeant. "They'll be swarming like hornets now," reasoned the company commander.

A detachment of rebel cavalry rode into view at the far end of the meadow. The cannons roared again just as two more shells burst in front of the Southern Troopers. "You just can't break in on a man's breakfast," quipped Gormley.

"That sure would be enough to get my dander up," the captain agreed.

A detachment of Union Cavalry arrived and formed to the regiments left. The federal captain readied his sword and un-holstered his pistol. "I'll bet a month's pay we're in for more than a wee scrap," said the Top Sergeant. "Yep, we'll be shoulder high in gray before this day get's much older," Andrew reasoned.

The Confederate Cavalry began to move forward at a walk.

A fusillade of cannon shot exploded amidst the horse soldiers. Three beasts and their riders dropped to the ground. One animal kicked wildly in the air. The rebels began to trot, quickening their pace as they moved forward. Another barrage landed to their front showering man and beast with falling debris. A gray clad officer moved to the front of his troops waving his sword. Suddenly, the whole line broke into a gallop. An instant later that famous Rebel yell screeched across the field.

The union captain moved in front of his troop and calmly raised his sword. He pointed the blade forward while quickening his pace to a trot. "My God Captain there's a sight the likes I've never seen," Sergeant Gormley exclaimed.

Just then the Blue clad Horse Soldiers broke into a gallop adding their own screaming voices to the din. The men of the Fourteenth watched in fascination as the charging horseman drew inevitably closer.

Thirty yards separated the columns when men on each side fired their pistols. They rode into the drifting smoke where man and beast collided fiercely into their adversaries. Suddenly blue forms mixed with gray as they grappled in the center of the field.

Through the lifting haze the rebel captain cut a federal private out of his saddle with his saber. The confederate officer's horse is struck on the flanks and began to stagger. Unfazed, the rebel officer steadied his steed and slashed another bluebelly off his mount.

The union color bearer and his confederate counterpart wheeled and struck at each other with their swords. Managing to hold one hand on there respective flags.

A southern sergeant engaged the federal captain. They flailed viciously at each other with their swords. The gray clad trooper slashed into the union officer's left arm causing him to falter. Finally, the rebel charged into the federal commander slashing him from his horse. The wounded Officer shoots the Sergeant before falling from a stray bullet. The union color bearer and his counterpart have dragged each other from their mounts. They battled on the ground with sabers. The butternut standard bearer rushed wildly at his adversary slashing with his sword,

but the Bluebelly parry's the attack
and felled the man with his saber.

The union cavalrymen are being
slowly beaten back. The color bearer
is shot. As he falls another blue clad
horse soldier retrieves the flag. The
federal bugler blows recall and they
fall back to regroup.

The red egged Troopers of the
Fourteenth fell back into their positions. "Ready men," Andrew shouted,
"We'll be receiving rebel horse in a
bit." Sure enough the rebel captain
wheeled his troop into position. The
line of gray clad horsemen yelled in
unison as they charged directly into
their enemy. "Hold on men we'll hit em
with a volley when they get to that
fence post" Gormley shouted. The confederate troopers are into a full gallop as they approach Andrew's position. The rebel captain raised his
sword and pointed it straight ahead as
they thunder closer to the fence post.
"Give it to em," screamed the Brooklyn
sergeant.

A fusillade of shot smashed into
the flesh of man and beast. Dozens of
gray clad troopers are knocked to the
ground, rider less horses scatter into
the underbrush. The Rebel standard

bearer is among the first casualties. Another butternut takes possession of the flag as it falls.

"Lay another one into them" shouted the fiery Andrew. No sooner had he spoke than a volley of lead hit the screaming secessionists causing their whole line to falter.

More than a dozen enemy soldiers crash blindly into the dirt. The screeching of crazed animals becomes mixed with the sounds of battle. Some of the dazed creatures trail their entrails as they stagger about.

The confederate captain raced into their position. He slashed one trooper and wounded another with his pistol. It is a brawl at close quarters that is favored by the redlegged Infantrymen. Gormley knocked a butternut from a horse with the butt of his rifle. Another reb leveled his pistol at him, but the husky sergeant grabbed his arm and flung him to the ground.

It is a wild donnybrook with men flailing hard at each other. Wild eyed horses kicking and prancing about added to the melee.

The rebel commander attacked Andrew knocking him to the ground. Captain Whelan jumped to his feet, took the horse by the bridle and began swinging the animal in circles. The mounted Rebel attempted to slash him with his saber, but the horse staggered and fell. Crawling out from under the critter the confederate officer rushed at his counterpart wielding his saber. The angered Andrew dispatched the man with a thrust of his bayonet.

Now, it is the rebel bugler blowing recall. Confederate cavalry break off the action to gallop off the field.

Some of their unhorsed brethren follow behind on foot. Union artillery exploded on the field as the butternuts disappear into the tree line.

"Well, we've blooded their hides a bit, but we're a nosing our way back to Pennsylvania. Can ye tell me what the Johnnies are up to," Gormley gasped. "I reckon only Robert E. Lee can answer that, sergeant. He's been looking to do battle on Union soil," Captain Whelan replied.

CHAPTER ELEVEN

As Dolan's wagon train passed through
the Keystone State the lads become more
aware of the turmoil. There seemed to
be a collective air of apprehension
in the population. Although watching
many military wagons rolling to and
fro would cause worry to most cit-
izens. Also clearly evident was the
mass of troops passing through their
towns and villages. Hastily formed
militia Regiments in all shades of
blue were camped in many Pennsylvania
fields these days. What aroused the
runaway's attention were the artillery
caissons moving with armed guards sitting abreast the cannons. "Doggone it
Will we're getting darn close to seeing a real battle after all," Bobby
exclaimed. "Sure is more soldiers
around than I ever hoped to see" his
friend answered. Young Whelan seemed
content watching his excited companion

react to this new life they were thrust
into. He enjoyed the way his side kick
took charge of the wagon. Will knew
from the beginning his friend was good
with his hands. He had the sloping
rounded shoulders of a prize fighter,
but of late he realized his partner
was coming of age. "Hard to believe
all this going on," Bobby remarked."
Those big cannon just a slogging up
the road as easy as you please," he
added. "Whatever it is that's gonna
happen we're right there in it," Will
responded. "It raises the hair on my
neck just thinking about it," said the
Ambrose boy. "It's gonna take some plan-
ning to shake loose of Dinky," young
Whelan remarked. Yep, he thought, the
wily muleskinner always watched them
closely. The Irishman needed them to get
where he was going. They would have to
jump at a moments notice to make their
getaway. "He'll lock us up for sure if
he just thinks we're looking to mosey
off somewhere," Bobby said in a hushed
voice. The sly old Dinky had a way of
popping up when a guy least expected
it. They woke up one morning and he was
setting there grinning at them with
those crooked snaggle teeth. "He sure
does like to jingle those leg irons

under our noses," Will pointed out. His friend nodded his head in a knowing kind of way. "Yeah, and that parole business with those papers he keeps showing us," Bobby recalled. They both chuckled at how the tiny old Irishman threatened them. "He never does let us read what's in those papers. I'm thinking it's all some kind of fake," young Whelan contended.

A group of union cavalrymen led by a lieutenant and a corporal approached Dinky's wagons with their hands raised for him to stop. "You'll have to get those wagons off the road. We've got a column that needs to move through," explained the corporal. "Is that a fact, well, I've got me own troubles, I'll be a needing to move on meself your highness," was Dinky's sarcastic response. "Its Army orders sir" pleaded the trooper. "I'll not be dawdling here for the Bishop himself," Dinky screeched. The exasperated corporal gestured to the officer. "If he doesn't move have the men distribute his goods," ordered the lieutenant. "What will be your pleasure, sir," asked the grinning Trooper. "Ye've not heard the last of Dinky Dolan ye bloody rascals," The muleskinner growled, but he urged his team off the road. The irate Irishman pulled under a cluster of trees muttering a stream of unintelligible oaths about the birthright of union soldiers. He set his wheel brake with an angry jerk bringing his rig to an abrupt stop. Daniel and the boys pulled their wagons alongside, but the infuriated Dolan was beside himself with temper. He lashed the mules cruelly across their rumps in uncontrolled fury. Beating the critters for a full two minutes until his rage was exhausted. The black teenager climbed down from his buckboard moving in a slow deliberate manner.

He ambled over towards the spent Sutler looking much like a whipped puppy. "We gonna be camping here," Daniel uttered in a low submissive voice. "Put up the animals or you'll be next to feel me whip," shouted the very annoyed muleskinner. "The bloody army's clogging up the roads. We've little choice but wait for the bluebelly louts to move on." Dinky raved. The diminutive Irishman reached into his wagon and began throwing pots and pans onto the ground. He scaled metal plates high in the air combined with a handful of eating utensils. Daniel worked his way back to the runaways who were unable to suppress a grin. "Mister Dink says we gotta put up the animals and make camp," the Colored boy muttered. "I reckon he's mad at those soldier boys," Will declared still trying to control his laughter at the Irishman's antics. Daniel looked back to see if Dolan was still in his wagon before cracking a wide grin. "Ol Dinky's acting like a spoiled white boy who done dropped his sweet roll in a mud puddle," he whispered.

Later that evening the resilient Muleskinner was busily preparing Johnnie Cakes for troops from nearby encampments. In a complete turnabout from his earlier action he was humming an Irish tune and tap dancing around the fire. No doubt the thought of filling his pockets with Yankee money improved his disposition. The teenagers were helping him stack the hot cakes on a side grill. By now the smell of bacon had drawn a long line of prospective customers. Two sergeants, one a barrel chest six striped top soldier, the other a three striper with a bushy red beard approached the muleskinner as he ladled dough onto the griddle. "That's right me buckoes step up and I'll feed ye the best Johnnie cakes ye've ever tasted," ain't that a fact Daniel," bragged the Irishman. The Black boy nodded yes while flashing his obedient eyes lowered grin. "They sure is the best cakes this side of Dixie," he replied. "What's the cost of a plate of those fritters?" asked the Top Soldier. Two dollars and ye can set ye jaw upon four sweet smelling pancakes," Dolan exclaimed. "A man can make a sack of money on a tiny bit of flour," the man remarked. "He could that" Dinky taunted with his snaggle toothed grin. "And there ain't a finer fellow than meself it can happen too," he added sarcastically. "I'm thinking a bank robber don't make the kind of money you're making," The Three Striper commented. "Ay, but he doesn't have to bother with a blowhard or two" was Dolan's derisive reply. "That's the trouble with most of you sutler's you run off your mouths too much," red beard sneered. "Ah, yes, me dear old mom said I'd be better off with me lips sewed shut," replied the tiny Irish merchant. "You'd be better off if you moved down the road," The Top kick joined in. "Ah, but ye have me baffled now. Is it off the road or on the road ye want me?" Dolan inquired, his voice dripping with venom. The Six Striper moved his large frame closer to the short argumentative Muleskinner. He put a crooked finger on the point of Dolan's nose. "If I was you I'd close up your mess now. You're not a Sutler for this regiment," he shouted. "Ay, I'm not, Governor John A. Andrew of the Commonwealth of Massachusetts commissioned me as a Sutler I'll have ye know," Dinky responded with obvious pride. The Three Striper moved in and grabbed the Muleskinner tightly by the collar raising him off the ground. "Well, go and find one of those Massachusetts regiments afore I break your dirty neck," he shouted. The sergeant dropped the tiny Irishman and he stumbled backwards to regain his balance. "I will that and it won't be soon enough," was the chastened Dolan's reply. He looked back at the line of Soldiers who were beginning to disperse into the night, a grumbling lot of blue coats returning hungry to their tents. Dinky kicked dirt on the fire and drank heartily from his jug. He flung pot and pans in all directions cursing his luck.

The outraged Irishman continued to sip Applejack. The teenagers returned to their tents to bed down for the night. "Ol Dinky's getting his self fired up on demon rum," muttered the Colored boy. They peered through the tent flap to watch the muleskinner scatter cooking utensils into the darkness. Finally, the drunken Irishman staggered to his feet. "Come and get it Sergeants I've a fine piece of leather for ye" Dolan screeched into the moon lit night. He snapped his whip in the air casting weird shadows as he stumbled about. "C'mon ye bloody cowards I'll lay a stripe on ye arm ye'll carry to ye grave," Dolan ranted, stumbling into a large forsythia bush. "Where are ye now ye bunch of blackards come out and fight," dared the tiny Irishman freeing himself from the entangled branches. Dinky took another huge swig from his mug before placing it and the whip on the ground. Striking a fighters pose he swung wildly with his fists at an imagined enemy. I'll fight ye with me hands if ye dare show ye faces," railed the drink soused muleskin-ner. The lads watched in fascination as Dolan tottered in circles swinging wild punches at his own shadow. "Ay's a feared Mister Dink's done lost his mind," Daniel groaned.

"I think he's just crazy drunk," Bobby whispered. They huddled together not knowing what the man was capable of in that condition. "Come out of the tent lads I've a surprise for ye," Dolan pleaded. They inched further away from the entrance flap. "Are ye gonna do as I say, Daniel, or do I come in there after ye," he snarled. "I don't know about y'all, but Dinky's after this black boy's hide," cried the intimidated lad. He gets you and he'll have to get us all, right Will?" the Ambrose boy promised.

"Yep, I reckon that's the way it has to be. I'd give a quarter to see those sergeants come moseying up the road," his side kick replied.

The incensed muleskinner began lashing the canvas with his whip. "Come out or I'll stove ye bloody tent in," he railed. "I'll be a going outside afore he bashes it in," mumbled a resigned Daniel. "Nope, we're all going out together," shouted the determined Bobby. "We's a coming out Mister Dink!" the colored boy exclaimed scooting next to his leader. The runaways moved to either side of their friend. "Take off

ye shirts the lot of ye," shrieked the
sullied Irishman. He tottered forward
snapping the leather thong across the
black boy's shoulder. "You better stop
that Mister Dolan. There's no reason
for you to use a whip on us," Will
maintained in a loud clear voice. "I'll
bare ye back bared to the bone ye bloody
devil," The Irishman shouted swinging
the whip at young Whelan. The rangy
lad ducked under the lunging Merchant
as Bobby led the Black boy aside. "Oh,
it's the three of ye is that what yer
telling me?" screamed the enraged
Dolan. "Get yerself over here nigrah,"
he ordered snapping his whip menacingly across a tree stump. "Stay where
you are Daniel," insisted the faithful
Bobby in a no nonsense tone. "Are ye
willing to bare ye fists against Dinky
Dolan mister prize fighter?" the wee
man shouted. He threw the whip to the
ground and raised his hands to back up
the challenge. "Get em up if yer man
enough," Dared the Merchant. "I don't
want to fight you Mister Dolan," The
lad contended.

"To be sure it won't be much of a
brawl ye beggar," he grinned. "C'mon
me lad don't tell me be yer afraid of

dear old Dolan?" taunted the snaggle toothed muleskinner.

But instead, the Irishman rushed headlong into Daniel knocking him to the dirt. "Box him Bob show em what you're made of," Will hollered angered by the man's taunting. Dinky rushed at the younger Whelan, but his friend moved in to cut him off. "That's it me buckoe come and get it," grinned the wizened Muleskinner. "Stay on your toes Bob he can't hit you when you move," advised his side kick. Dolan swung wildly, but the agile youngster easily danced away. The lad continued to circle and the Irishman resorted to head down bull like rushes.

"Stay put and fight ye blasted little devil," shouted the exasperated merchant. Once again Dinky lunged, but the boy grabbed him under the armpit and flipped him to the ground. "Would ye help a poor old man to his feet," asked the cagy sutler. Bobby extended his hand to pull him to his feet. Dolan threw a roundhouse right just missing Bobby's jaw. "He can't hit nothing but air," laughed his excited friend. "I'll show ye what I can hit," screeched the exhausted Irishman. He charged head-first into his speedy opponent. Bobby took him by the shoulder and slammed him directly into the dust. The tired Muleskinner could barely drag himself to his feet. "Will ye stop ye dancing and give a man a fair fight," begged the winded Dolan. To the older man's credit or drunkenness he again rushed straight at his adversary with arms flailing. Bobby slipped his hand under Dolan's armpit to spill him flat on the ground. "This is some fight Daniel, Dinky can't hit Bobby and Bobby won't hit Dinky," Will observed.

Dinky tried to get back to his feet, but he couldn't make it. His nose began running blood onto his lips. "Ye've broken me nose." he moaned. "The very man who rescued ye from the coppers that's the thanks I get," wailed the wee Irish merchant. Daniel walked over to his long time friend to kneel by his side. "Y'all got yourself all tuckered out Mister Dink," drawled the Colored boy. "I'm dying Daniel. Will ye help old Dinky now that he's bashed and bleeding?" cried the wily old Muleskinner. Dolan's body heaved to and fro as he sobbed. Large tears streaked his blood stained face. The merchant was in a booze induced crying fit. "I didn't mean to hurt you none," declared the compassionate Bobby. "Ye've done me in lad I'll not see the light of another day," he whimpered. Dinky closed his eyes soaking up the sympathy. "Daniel you get his arms Bobby and I will take his legs. The black boy looked anxiously at Dolan, but followed Will's instructions. They carried the bedraggled merchant back to the campsite and placed him next to the still simmering fire. Stifling a laugh Will and Bobby located a full barrel of water and dragged it next to their prostrate leader. "About time Dinky had a bath," Will whispered. The runaways carefully removed the Irishman's outer clothing down to his long underwear. The colored boy backed away in disbelief, but grinned when he watched them dump the Irishman headfirst into the drum. "Oh, ye blasted traitors ye've no idea how bad water is to a grown man," he wailed. "Here's something to flavor up your bath Mister Dolan," Will quipped, sliding a bar of soap in the barrel.

CHAPTER TWELVE

The invading confederate army of northern Virginia some 75,000 strong had penetrated deep into Union soil. Robert E Lee set up Headquarters on a knoll near Sharpsburg,

Maryland. The general sat outside on a camp stool under a stretched canvas pondering strategy. The loss of Stonewall Jackson his most effective campaigner weighed heavily on the commanders heart. His old war Horse lieutenant general James Longstreet was the only experienced corps commander left to him. The general would have to be everywhere if he wanted his plans to be carried out.

Lee watched his aide guide a civilian gentleman along the winding path leading to his command center. The general rose to his feet as they stepped under the overhang.

"Mister Leghorn wanted to deliver this himself," grinned the aide. The tall weather beaten man dressed in blue overalls and obviously a farmer stepped forward to present a colander of raspberries to the southern leader. "Why thank you sir I'll have then with lunch," said the surprised Lee as he accepted the man's offering. "I'm not in sympathy with your cause, but I'd be mighty obliged if you would write your name down on a piece of paper so I could show it to my friends," He requested in a loud clear voice. "Don't you think it could be dangerous to possess the autograph of a well-known rebel," quipped the confederate commander. "I'm a true union man, but I'll take my chances carrying the name of Robert E. Lee in my pocket," farmer Leghorn responded. "I see you're as firm in your principles as I am mine," acknowledged the general. Returning to his field desk he signed his name on a parchment and handed it to the man. "Thank you sir," grinned the loyalist. He peered at the paper for a moment as you would a painting or a work of art. Without a gesture or another word he turned and left.

The concerned general turned to watch the local land owner saunter down the path. "Our Army moves through their countryside yet the people seem relatively calm," observed the aide. "The conduct of our soldiers is of utmost importance we will not tolerate the perpetration of barbarous outrages against civilians," declared the southern commander. "There have been a few instances of looting, but on the whole our men have shown remarkable prudence," the officer was quick to assert. "It must be remembered we make war on armed men. We shall not take vengeance for the wrongs our own people have suffered without lowering ourselves in the eyes of all," stated Lee. "The general order covering the conduct of all individual soldiers has been explained to all commands," the aide confirmed. The commander peered out over the rolling hills shading his eyes from the sun with one hand. "The richness of this valley and the wealth of its people are puzzling to our troops. They'd like to dip their hands into this troth," observed the taciturn southern field commander. "A Court Martial hanging over a man's head is at least a deterrent," the aide replied. "Supplies must be taken by formal requisition. If our confederate money is refused issue receipts for the seized property in fair market value," General Lee explained.

On the left wing of the southern advance general John B. Hood and his mounted staff led their bedraggled Division through a small Hamlet near Chambersburg. Groups of civilians lined the streets while others leaned out windows, or sat nonchalantly on open porches. "Half you Reb's won't have to worry about walking back this way again," shouted a one legged union veteran leaning on crutches. "The other half's gonna be toting Yankee lead in their rear ends," laughed a voice from a window. A bare headed confederate soldier removed a hat from a bystander and placed it on his head. "Hell johnnie I'd have given you my hat if you asked. You'll be chasing crows out of the cornfields afore long," he commented. Yes, they were a haggard looking bunch of scarecrows these Texas Infantrymen, but some of the fiercest fighters in the world. "Y'all will be whistling Dixie next time we come marching by," hollered a tall ragged

rebel corporal. "Oh yeah, that sorry
looking bunch ain't likely to make it
where they're headed never mind back,"
shouted a store proprietor leaning
against a crate of yams.

"Ain't no bluebelly army ever stopped
us yet," wailed a bespectacled butternut. Another gray clad private grabbed
a bystander's hat to place it over his
matted hair. "Give them Bloody Secesh
your lids boys they got a heap of walking twixt here and Dixie," shouted
a teamster from his buckboard. "You
reckon we could get Ol Abe's topper
and give it to Jeff Davis," quipped a
long bearded Texas soldier.

In another tiny Pennsylvania town
not forty miles away Andrew led a
patrol consisting of his top kick,
Corporal Duffy and Private Henry. They
proceeded along a wagon road leading
to a farm community consisting of four
cottages and a barn. The surrounding area was dotted with small farms
typical of the Pennsylvania Quakers.
"A bright lad could settle down here
and raise a brood of tykes in country like this," Gormley remarked. "A
place where a straggler might want to
set out the war," the Captain added
in. "Ay, it is that," the top kick

agreed. As they approached the barn a federal officer stepped out to greet them. "I'm Lieutenant John Hoffman of the one hundred sixteenth Pennsylvania at your service, sir. There's a bunch of scalawags in that house up ahead. They're holding the family hostage," snapped the Lieutenant. "I'm captain Whelan, the fourteenth new York. I've a hunch they're the deserters we've been asked to corral", Andrew quickly responded. Gormley motioned the detachment to take cover with the lieutenant's compliment of one corporal and five privates. The men unlimbered their muskets and joined their counterparts.

In the farmhouse four unkempt bedraggled looking union soldiers held an Amish farmer, his wife and two teenage daughter's hostage. Two of the stragglers including their leader a burly lumberjack are from the sixth Michigan. The other two are both members of the second New Jersey. The family is huddled in the kitchen. Three of the rogues are posted at windows with rifles ready. The leader sat at the kitchen table tossing his knife at the floor. "Doggone it man get some food on the table. Ain't you the kind of folks who just love your neighbors to death," shouted the chief scoundrel. "Get mama's bread und the ham. Ve haf food ve give food," said the father. The obedient girls rushed to a nearby cupboard. The Wife reached under a counter for a pail of milk. Minutes later the bright cheeked daughters were cutting slabs of ham while their mother filled pitchers with cream.

Seeing this the three lookouts rushed to the table to join in the feast. "You got something besides milk, maybe some homemade whiskey or wine," asked the former woodcutter.

"Ve haf no spirits, spring vater and milk is all," replied the farmer. His one daughter filled glasses with water while the other distributed them. "Und maybe a fraulein to help a man mit his laundry," mocked the chief rogue. "Yeah, he ain't washed his duds since Chancellorsville," remarked the other Michigan thug. "He wants to look purty for the hanging," snarled one of the jersey brigands. "Gotta catch a man afore they swing him," sneered the other.

"That squad down the road is fixing the noose right now," chuckled their leader,

Andrew assembled his own men with the Lieutenant's soldiers inside the barn. "Men, we're going to show those deserters army discipline at its best. We'll be marching up to that house in formation with arms shouldered; much like you did in training," declared the tall captain. "Those scalawags are, err, armed sir," the junior officer pointed out. "They're union soldier's lieutenant that's what I'm counting on. We'll give them rascals something to think about. I want one man to circle that house and move in when we get close. Any volunteers," asked the Red Legged Company Commander. Andrew grinned widely when the entire detachment stepped forward. "I've got rank here over the enlisted lads anyway's and I've a little rank I want to pull on the scoundrels," Insisted the first sergeant. Not waiting for an answer the top kick rushed out of the enclosure to begin his mission. They watched him run to a heavily wooded area adjacent the house where he disappeared into the foliage.

Inside the building the rogues have piled furniture behind the front windows and leveled their rifles on the road. Andrew's detachment moved out of the barn in rows of two. They marched in perfect order up the path with the tall company commander in the lead. "They're coming up the road," shouted the Michigan deserter. The burly leader peered at the oncoming union troopers in disbelief. "The doggone fools are marching up the street like the British," he exclaimed. "And a pair of Red Pants in the lead," added the rascal from New Jersey. "Like tin soldiers on parade," he added.

Sergeant Gormley crawled to a large apple tree at the side of the house. He broke into a grin as he watched his Commander advance straight at his objective. "God love ye captain for the dam fool that ye are," he whispered.

The scalawags meanwhile are unsure of their next move. "They're getting close it's either cut out or cut loose," the jittery New Jersey man hollered. "Fire a volley over their heads," ordered their leader. The Rogues pushed their rifles through the window and fired.

There is no mistaking the crack of a bullet over a seasoned veterans head, but Andrew never wavered in his line of march. "Easy men they're just trying to scare us off," he said in a steady voice. "My knees ain't ever gonna stop knocking," Private Henry exclaimed.

Gormley reached the rear door just as the Scalawags have finished reloading their muskets. "Give em another one," shouted the burly former Lumberjack. The four muskets exploded in unison sending their missiles whistling above their targets.

Three of his men falter but captain Whelan urges them on. "Keep your pace men those rounds were all high," the quick stepping officer persisted. "The captain got more nerve than a bank robber," cried a frightened Pennsylvania private.

Amidst all this commotion the top kick managed to enter the house through the rear door. He pressed forward until he spotted two of the deserters in the next room. Gormley crouched low inching his way to gain a better view.

Finally, he observed the hostages huddled together against a large cupboard. Another scalawag is partially visible behind a stacked wooden table. The rogue leader stood by a narrow window peering at the oncoming patrol. "Put one into that front rank," he shrieked. "Don't be a dam fool all they got us for is desertion," pleaded his associate.

"I'm gonna get me an officer," he growled back. Sergeant Gormley stepped into the room as the deserter was leveling his rifle at Andrew. "Put ye bloody rifles on the deck," the top kick ordered, cocking his musket. "You'll have to take mine" replied the burly lumberjack. The desperado turned from the window and snapped off a shot, but it slammed into a door buck. Gormley dropped him dead with a ball through the chest. The other rogues discarded their rifles as the detachment bust through the front door. "The others were giving up, but that misguided rascal wanted to part ye hair captain," the sergeant explained pointing to the prostrate scalawag leader. "Not a bad bit of soldiering sergeant Gormley," the commanding officer grinned. "I'll not mention that wee stroll ye took these lads on up that garden path," quipped the top kick. They both chuckled, but Andrew realized the mission wasn't over. "Take those prisoners to the Provost Marshal," he said to the Lieutenant. "And give that man a decent burial," he added almost absentmindedly.

"Yes sir and I'd like to say this was one heck of a day," The young officer replied. Andrew surveyed the farm house with its broken windows and smashed furniture before turning to the farmer. "The army will reimburse you for any damage," he assured the man. "Thank you sir, but I do mine own work on mine own farm und I vetch army do its work on mine farm," replied the Dutchman. "Can't argue with a man who thinks like that," Andrew grinned.

CHAPTER THIRTEEN

On the Confederate right just North of Rockville, Maryland Jeb Stuart's Cavalry entered a town known to be sympathetic to the south. A company of union soldiers posted at a hastily erected road block opened fire on the approaching horse soldiers. The Rebels quickly charged the outpost cutting down eight of its defenders. After a quick battle the out manned federals were forced to surrender. The victorious rebels rode back to parade their banners through the city streets. The southern column passed a girls seminary where young women with hastily curled hair posed in windows. Another group of lady Seminarians burst from a doorway to mingle with the mounted Rebels. "Doggone shame we can't stop here a spell," cracked a smiling private. "Get down off those animals and let a girl see that gray uniform you're so proud of," cried a tall winsome blonde. The lady walked onto the road to pull at the mane of a strawberry roan ridden by a brash young lieutenant. The well decorated officer responded with a broad smile to the girls teasing.

Noticing a union mule train off in the distance one of Stewart's aides rode quickly to his side. "There goes a federal wagon train hightailing it back towards Washington," cried the excited officer. "Might just as well see what they're carrying, have a squadron follow us," the general ordered. The intractable rebel leader spurred his horse to a gallop with the aide motioning to a detachment to join them. They raced after the retreating enemy wagons closing the distance with each stride. With another spurt of speed the general pulled alongside the rear cart. He was joined by a howling horde of veteran horse soldiers smelling bounty. The gray clad soldiers caused havoc amongst the union drivers. They collided with each other causing some to overturn. Mule's tore loose of their bindings to gallop blindly in all directions. Burn those overturned freighters," ordered Stuart. A detachment of troopers howled their delight as they torched the federal wagons. "They'll see that smoke in Washington," shouted a butternut captain.

"Cut those poles down" shouted the confederate general.

The whooping cavalrymen started a large bonfire by adding the telegraph posts to the burning supply wagons. Plumes of black smoke rose from the carnage.

Continuing his advance General Lee moved his staff headquarters into Pennsylvania. A dust stained confederate scout entered the command tent to file his report. As a precaution the general's aide checked the man's Identification papers. Satisfied they are authentic the officer returned them to their owner. "A mister John Harrison to see you sir," was the young subordinate's manner of introduction. "General Longstreet believes you have information regarding the Union positions," Lee inquired, pushing aside all formality. "I had a drink or two with the federals in Washington. Been chatting with union soldiers in the saloons by day and walking through their lines at night," The spy declared. "Do you know Hooker's position," queried the

General. "Yes, he crossed the Potomac
at Frederick City with two corps of
infantry. I heard of another corps
nearby, but couldn't find them," the
scout answered without a moments hesitation like someone sure of his facts.
The confederate commander appeared
surprised at what he heard. "Hooker's
on the North side of the Potomac close
to my rear and I have yet to hear from
Stewart. The eyes of my army are off
only God knows where," Lee lamented.
"On my way here I saw two more Corps at
South Mountain. Oh, yes, and I heard
Hooker's been replaced by Meade," the
Scout reported. "My old friend George
Meade, well, he'll make no blunder on
my front," declared the rebel leader.
"Will that be all general," the spy
asked. "Yes, Mister Harrison you've
provided some valuable information,"
Lee responded. The wizened infiltrator
tipped his hand to his cap in a weak
salute and left. But General Lee was
energized by the new turn of events.
He moved to his map board to ponder
his action. "The advance on Harrisburg
must be abandoned we must consolidate
our forces," murmured the concerned
rebel leader. "Shall I ready orders
for morning dispatches," queried the

aide. "No, this is of immediate importance have couriers ride to each command we're too far afield.

The enemy will find us or we'll find
them here. Lee pointed to the towns of
Cashtown and Gettysburg.

Shadowing the confederate invasion the federal forces have set up
operations on a wagon road outside
of Frederick Maryland. Major general
George G. Meade commanding General of
the Army of the Potomac sat inside his
headquarters tent enjoying his morning coffee. Captain James McHugh hurried through the tent flap and handed
him a dispatch. "Stuart's cavalry have
cut the telegraph wires near a town
called Sykesville," declared the staid
Commander. The subordinate walked over
to the camp table to thumb through a
series of maps. "That's about thirty
miles from the Capitol," McHugh stated
peering at the charts. Major General
Alfred

Pleasonton the cavalry commander
of the army of the Potomac brushed
through the canvas opening just as
Meade was about to speak. "Have you
heard about Stuart's raid on a town
called Sykesville not thirty miles
from Washington," queried the Union

Commander. "Good, that'll keep him from helping Lee," Pleasonton exclaimed slapping his glove against his leg for emphasis. "He's cut the telegraph wires," the concerned Meade remarked. "Perfect, George, now you can do what you dam well please," the cavalry commander was quick to point out. "You could take your cavalry and engage him," the senior officer implied. Pleasonton moved to the map board to trace the enemy's movements on the charts.

"Stuart's in a useless position. He must re-cross the Potomac if Lee needs help or he must ride North around our entire army. Leave him alone time is his enemy," snapped the brash horse soldier. "Makes darn good sense to me, but my concerns are with Lee. With both our armies heading north when will he turn and fight," asked the Union's Commanding General. "Yes, and where," Pleasonton replied still studying the maps.

CHAPTER FOURTEEN

Dinky Dolan's wagon train has once again been sidetracked by an army roadblock. Daniel and the runaways bunched together in one wagon watching the seemingly endless line of soldiers and equipment moving towards the war front. While the Muleskinner sat fuming on his buckboard awaiting permission to move ahead.

Militia units sporting different shades of blue and wearing dissimilar hats trudge awkwardly up the highway. Civilians from the nearby town of York offer the soldiers food and drams of cider. Veteran soldiers manning the roadblock snickered at the nattily dressed Militiamen. "Some Johnny Reb's gonna put a ball in those fancy duds," cracked a bearded Corporal. "Those Secesh will have those clothes off you afore you hit the ground," laughed a grizzled bluebelly.

A very angry Dolan stepped off his wagon to speak to the troopers manning the barricades. "Are ye ever gonna let a man go on his way," he asked a top sergeant. "Cant rightly tell when," he replied. "I'll have ye know I've been commissioned a sutler by the governor of the commonwealth of Massachusetts," stated the irate Irishman. "The only thing that'll get you on this road is a commission in the U. S. Army Mister Sutler," cracked the trooper. The soldier ambled away, but the persistent Dolan sidled alongside. "But it's me own regiment I'm looking for me buckoe. The lads are up ahead a wee bit," reasoned the wily merchant. "What's up ahead is Robert E, Lee. He's come busting down the Chambersburg Pike with the whole doggone reb army," countered the sergeant. "The devil you say and me with a bad back," answered the suddenly humble Irishman. "If I was you I wouldn't be rushing up that road. They'll be letting you through soon enough," was the man's earnest warning.

The chastened Dinky nodded his head in resignation, but returned to confer with the teenagers. "A fine lot of malarkey this on and then off the road again business is.

That's what the army is lads a fine lot of malarkey," wailed the Wee Irishman. "That's what they is for sure Mister

Dink," agreed the compassionate Colored boy. "Denying a man an honest living is what they are," the Muleskinner persisted while pounding his fist into his bowler hat.

"Seems like they're trying to do what's right for everybody," Bobby interjected. "Sure and I knew you'd be siding against Dolan," snarled the Muleskinner. "Bobby's right, the army's just doing what it needs to do," the

Whelan boy pointed out. "I'd have expected a bit of loyalty from the pair of ye," Dinky whined in exasperation.

But as they spoke the military traffic began to subside.

The Sergeant manning the roadblock waved for the driver of the first wagon to move out onto the road. "Get to ye wagons ye beggars we're off again and it's about time," he screeched. The boys hopped back in their carts as Dinky began to move ahead. Minutes later their wagons were mixed with civilian carriages of all sorts. Will remained silent for a moment contemplating their situation, but he knew they soon had to break loose of Dolan. "We'll have to be making our own way before long partner," said the lanky teenager.

"You reckon the regiment is close by?" his partner queried.

"Can't rightly say where they are," Will reasoned, but he sure did want to know where his brother Andrew was. "Old Dinky's gonna get the Pinkerton's after us that's for sure," said the concerned Ambrose lad. "It won't be easy finding us with all this army out here," were his sidekicks reassuring words.

To Dinky's chagrin a large group of army wagons from the second New Jersey moved up and began passing him by.

Another group of soldiers led by a union major pulled up alongside Dinky's wagon. "Pull those wagons off the road," the officer shouted. "And who is it that ye think ye are? Get off the road indeed," was the Irishman's sarcastic reply.

"My orders are to clear the road of all civilians if necessary," explained the major. "I'm an army sutler I'll have ye know Dolan railed. "I see by your markings what you are, but orders are the same get those wagons off the road," The trooper repeated. "I'll not move me wagons off this road again for the Pope himself," screeched the wee Irishman. The major waved to a nearby lieutenant who rushed to his side. "Have a few of your men ride through the Sutler's wagon," he thundered for all to hear. The Major wheeled his mount in a display of horsemanship before riding off in a cloud of dust. The lieutenant spurred his own horse back to a detachment of soldiers shouting instructions. Three wagons each with four troopers on board immediately rushed to the Dolan wagon train. They lifted the runaways off the buckboard and placed them on the ground. Moments later Daniel stood open mouthed watching the blue clad troopers shift goods from his wagon to there's. The joyous soldiers threw kegs of Dinky's home made Applejack to other passing units who accepted them willingly. The incensed muleskinner jumped from his wagon and ran back to confront the soldiers. "Stop it ye bloody bunch of burglars," he shouted. "Have ye all gone daft," the outraged merchant railed. Another cart full of troopers stopped by to check what the commotion was all about. A tall light haired

sergeant from the second New Jersey
looked straight into Dolan's face and
peered into the Irishman's pale blue
eyes. The man turned to a Corporal sitting next to him and hollered "Do you
know who that Is," The thick muscled
two striper nodded his head in recog-
nition. "I sure do it's that sutler
from the tenth Massachusetts, the one
who put that doggone lump on my head,"
he replied jumping to the ground. But
the Sergeant was first to reach the
wee Irishman. He grabbed Dinky by his
coat and raised him off the ground.
"It has to be the lord who put you in
my hands," growled the top kick.

   "You wouldn't want him all to yourself now?" asked the two striper,
edging closer all the time. "No, a
gift like this has to be shared," the
Sergeant was quick to agree. He swung
Dolan like a rag doll into the other
Troopers arms. "I wonder what he's got
in his britches?" laughed the corporal. He grabbed Dinky by the ankles
shaking him violently until everything
in his pockets including a bulging
change purse fell to the roadway. "See
what happens when you coddle a man,"
cracked the top kick. He watched his
partner tear Dolan's leather poke in

pieces allowing the gold coins to settle in the palm of his hand.

"That's me own private property I'll have ye know," cried the
Irishman. Hearing that remark the
husky two striper bounced the squirm-
ing Muleskinner's head off the ground.

"It looks like the gold I lost a
couple of weeks back," the sergeant
pointed out. "It sure does, I remember seeing a few of those shiny pieces
close up," his companion agreed. He
swung the muleskinner like a pendulum
for a moment just letting his victim
thrash about like a bird trying to
take flight. "Hard to reckon with a man
who'd feed you moonshine afore pinching
your poke", the top kick remarked in
a voice full of loathing. "He's a sly
old fox that's for sure," replied the
two striper. "Okay, pull those wagons
off the road," boomed the sergeant to
his waiting subordinates. They reacted
instantly, nudging the carts from the
right of way. "Are we gonna give the
Sutler that treat we were talking
about," asked the corporal. "Yep, I've
been a promising this to myself if
we ever caught up with this thieving
rascal," the trooper in charge said
emphatically. He reached down to grab

Dolan by the coat and ripped one of the sleeves off. His partner ripped the other one off. "Have ye taken leave of ye senses," Dinky wailed. Hearing that cry they ripped the remainder of his coat in two pieces. "A fine way to treat a man loyal to the union," moaned the Irishman. The man says he's a patriot," laughed the two striper mocking the wily merchant. "We're gonna leave you like you left us mister loyal union man," promised the top kick. Together the soldiers ripped Dinky's shirt from his back. "I'll be doggoned if he ain't a scrawny looking runt," chuckled the stocky Corporal. "The man could use a good bath," his partner concluded. Once again they bounced the wee Irishman's head off the ground to a round of cheers from the gathered Troopers. "Let's see how many knots we can put on the crooks noggin," cracked the top kick. "Can't say we ain't paid the sutler what we owed him," quipped his partner. They gave Dolan one final bounce in the dirt leaving him prostate on the road. The victorious troopers climbed back in their wagons and were off down the road to roars of laughter from their companions.

Daniel and the runaways were completely befuddled by the ferocity of the union soldiers. They also realized the muleskinner had brought this upon himself. The compassionate colored boy could restrain himself no longer. He worked his way towards Dolan and knelt down by his side. "Mister Dink," he whispered. Getting no reply he moved in closer to the unconscious Irishman and repeated "Mister Dink its Daniel, y'all better get up." By then the boys closed to within a few feet of the groaning Muleskinner. "I was you I'd get him some water," Will suggested looking into Dolan's bruised and bloody face. The black boy rushed to his wagon and returned with a canteen. He poured the clear liquid on the rag Bobby handed him as Will raised Dinky's head. Daniel dabbed the wet cloth on the muleskinner's face trying to revive him. "They just plain out whipped him like a dog," stated the shocked Ambrose lad. "Mister Dink y'all gotta get up them soldiers done gone down the road," cried the frightened colored boy. Will took hold of the canteen and emptied it on Dolan's face. "Have ye nothing but water to douse

a man with," Dolan groaned sputter-
ing his distaste of that clear liquid.
"They's gone and took all the goods
Mister Dink," Drawled his helper. But
the Wee Irishman was still groggy from
the beating he sustained. He slumped
down in the dirt mumbling an unintelligible Irish oath. The three friends
assisted the hapless Muleskinner to a
group of trees. They laid him down in a
large clump of Purple heather. "C'mon,
let's get the wagons over here so we
can set up camp," Will, shouted. An
instant later they were on the carts
and moving them into place. Daniel
grabbed some loose kindling while the
Runaways set up their canvas shelters.

Later that night the revived
Muleskinner sat by the fire nursing
his wounds. His black side kick was
sorting through pieces of army uniform
searching for something Dolan could
wear. "A fine lot of plunderers that's
what they are robbing an honest merchant of his goods," cried Dolan as he
dabbed a wet rag at his bruised chin.
"Ay's got four dollars you can have
Mister Dink," Daniel declared jingling
a pocketful of coins. "It ain't no
business of mine Mister Dolan, but you
did those soldiers first," declared the

Ambrose boy. "I'd have expected nothing
else from law abiding lads the likes
of you two escaped convicts," sneered
the wily merchant. "Can't say it any
better than Bobby did, but the plain
truth is we haven't did a thing we'd be
sorry for," the Whelan boy pointed out.
"Why don't ye get on ye way the sweet
angels that ye are. Taking me food and
grub and pretending to be me friends,"
was the Muleskinners scolding reply.
"I reckon we worked for what you gave
us and we'd surely been on our way cept
for that parole business," responded
the always candid Bobby. Dinky burst
out laughing holding his aching ribs
as his body shook with mirth. "Two
smart lads like yeselves and ye didn't
know ye were being led down the garden
path," he howled. The perplexed Ambrose
boy turned to his partner and asked
"What's he mean Will?" But his friend
shook his head in an all too familiar I told you so manner. "He's saying
it was all a fake," was his reluctant
reply. Bobby got up on his haunches so
he could look right into Dinky's face.
"We signed your papers in blood Mister
Dolan was that a fake too," queried
the very indignant Ambrose lad. "It
wasn't all that dumb, you got us down

the road this far," Will interjected.
"You sure did, right down that err,
path you're always talking about,"
Bobby chimed in. "Sure and you'll be
on yer way without so much as a tip
of ye hat to Dinky Dolan," cried the
crafty Irishman. "That ain't so Mister
Dolan we're sort of obliged to you,"
differed the dark haired runaway. "And
you too Daniel," Will chipped in.

"You White folks sure is funny.
Can't tell if y'all's fighting or fuss-
ing, doggoned if I can," drawled the
black boy. The muleskinner chuckled at
that remark holding his sides against
the pain. The runaways also burst out
laughing for a moment, but the wis-
dom of their colored friend's remark
caused them to fall silent in reflec-
tion. They did become full-fledged
muleskinners over these recent weeks.
Come tomorrow they would be on their
own again.

CHAPTER FIFTEEN

The runaways were almost hidden amidst a rolling tide of traffic, but they've become accustomed to all that frenetic activity. They walked the side of the highway oblivious to this general movement of the army. The young boys who escaped Saint John's home have changed somewhat. One can see it in their walk, or the confident way in which they swing their arms. "I just don't abide us up and leaving Daniel like that," confessed the Ambrose boy. He's where he needs to be, no sense fretting about that" Will reasoned, knowing his partner would never be convinced of that fact.

"You reckon that's really the way it is," his friend asked.

Will pondered that question for a moment before answering. "Dinky's a scalawag we know that for sure, but he's all the family Daniel's known" he pointed out. "It's the darndest thing I've ever seen" declared Bobby. Nope, he never would understand how a rascal like Dolan could receive such loyalty from an honest kid like Daniel.

At that very moment the black boy was sifting through the wagons determining what remained. "It's all lost me buckoe them bluebellies took every ounce of flour," Dinky declared.

"That's why you done sent those boys away cause you couldn't feed them, I knows that," Daniel murmured.

"A fine lot of nonsense that is," chuckled the unconvincing sutler. "Ay's a feared those boys is gonna get theyselves all shot up mister Dink," sobbed the concerned colored lad. "Ahh, but they've got a lot of brass the pair of them, marching off to war just as easy as pulling on ye britches," grinned the Wee Irishman as he peered wistfully down the crowded road.

But as they spoke in a meadow not two miles away the lads had settled on the course of action they were bound to pursue. They were approaching an army wagon manned by a youngish looking Captain Richard Daly of the One Hundred Sixteenth Pennsylvania. Standing to the officer's right was his top sergeant

a burly Dutchman named Rudolph Langer.
The soldiers were accepting volunteers
to field a company of militia. A group
of inquisitive farmers and field hands
were gathered nearby. "Anyone who
wants to fight the Reb's just sign up
and fall in behind this here wagon,"
the Captain explained to the crowd. A
tall red headed freckle faced boy moved
next to the runaways and extended his
hand. "My name's Tad Collins I'm fixing to join up how's about you," said
the friendly farm boy. "Yep, my friend
Bobby and I been looking to find an
outfit, but it looks like we'll just
up and join where we're needed," the
Whelan boy replied. "Oh yeah, and my
name is Will," he interjected. The red
haired boy stepped forward to shout
"I'll go if you're giving out muskets." The crowd laughed nervously at
this request. "There's a new Spencer
for any man willing to fight for
Pennsylvania," promised the officer.
"How's about uniforms," roared a voice
from the crowd. "Yep, regulation army
issue," replied the Captain. "I'll be
doggoned if I didn't always want to
fire one of those repeater rifles,"
admitted the freckle faced boy. The
boys followed Tad as he proceeded to

the front of the group. Sergeant Langer opened a ledger book and placed it on a camp table. "I heard those Johnnies been a carting off all the bluebellies they catch to Andersonville," cracked a farmer in bib overalls. "I heard they ain't taking any prisoners at all," snapped another field hand. "Ya sure und vat you wiseacres gonna say ven those Rebels come run you off your farm?" the burly top kick roared back. "The sergeant's right men the secesh are on our soil. They'll be in our fields eating our corn if we can't beat them back," the officer was quick to remind them.

More men responded to his words while others walked away grumbling. Just as Tad was getting ready to sign his name he looked at the top kick and said "I ain't never shot at a man afore, sergeant." The soldier hesitated a moment peering into the faces of those ready to fight for their beliefs.

"Ya, und never have I, maybe that's good und maybe that's bad," was his measured response.

An older gray headed slightly built man of fifty years stepped in next to the teenagers. "The name's Jonathan Marsh, lads I thought I might just volunteer my services," he said with a tip of his derby hat. Bobby was quick to accept the older man into the group. "This is my friend Will Whelan and this is Tad Collins. My name's Bobby Ambrose, glad to meet you sir" said the affable teenager. The boys stepped aside allowing the older man their spot in line. "I'd like to join your detachment," Jonathan declared. The sergeant gazed into the refined looking recruit's face taking notice of the determination in his eyes. "Und vy not" he snapped with a simple hand gesture. Tad stepped up and signed his name quickly handing the pen back to Will. The top kick looked the Whelan boy straight in the eye taking his measure no doubt. "Sixteen is your age," he asked in a no nonsense tone. "Yep," was all Will, could answer. Bobby took the pen and followed his partner's actions to the letter. To his surprise the soldier hardly looked at him. "Und you too is sixteen," he asked and waited for the expected "Yep," in reply. After signing their names each recruit was ushered to the rear of the wagon where they were assembled and loaded onto a large produce freighter. The wagon full of conscripts headed to an encampment not four miles away.

Twenty six green as grass would be troopers piled off that cart to await further instructions. Sergeant Langer approached the group wearing a subtle grin. "Line up by that quartermaster shack und you get your uniforms und rifles,"

He said, pointing to a dilapidated old pole barn. The enlistee's rushed forward anxiously, but Jonathon motioned for Tad and the runaways to stay back with him.

From the very beginning of the process everything had become hurried. It was almost comical watching those in the front catching the various items of clothing being flung at them. They had trousers, blankets, overcoats and socks draped over their outstretched arms. Some were trying to stuff clothing items into knapsacks and haversacks. Others laced shoes together and hung them around their necks. Canteens were stuffed into any available pocket. Everyone had a cap placed on his head whether it fit or not. A Spencer repeating rifle was thrust into each man's hand as he stepped out of the shanty. It was a dazed looking bunch of stragglers standing in the center of the company street loaded with newly issued gear.

Their new top kick came ambling around the side of the building to rescue the confused trainee's. "Come follow me," he said walking towards a row of tents. Like a covey of quail they fell in to the rear of their leader. When he reached the first tent he unceremoniously pushed four staggering would be soldiers through the entrance flap. He repeated the process until the line thinned to four. Then the Sergeant only pointed to the last dwelling. One could easily determine Jonathan was struggling to stand from the weight of his new equipment. The older man stumbled into the assigned domicile dropping pieces of clothing everywhere. Tad was dripping sweat, but he ambled in trying on his new issue cap. Bobby and Will were more excited about being in the Army than everyone else.

When they tried on their uniforms Bobby's hung on him like a scarecrow. His partners seemed to fit except the britches were loose. Jonathan's pants were hanging over his shoes his jacket is even larger and his shoes bigger yet.

"I'd be delighted if this uniform were a bit smaller," sighed the elder gentleman. "Shucks, mine fits like it was sewed on my back," countered the farm boy. Jonathan glanced at the smiling freckle faced boy in his snug union blue and said "I wish that I were so endowed." The red headed boy looked closely at his mature friend studying him carefully. "I don't know what you said, but the way you talk it wouldn't surprise me none if you was a school teacher," Tad speculated. "Are you really a teacher Jonathan," the Ambrose boy exclaimed. The genteel looking older man paused a moment as if searching for the proper way to answer the youngster. "That's a question better asked of my students," was his polite reply. "Can't reckon a teacher shouldering a musket," Will remarked while pulling on his new britches. "My home is twelve miles from here I will not be scared off my own land by southern rebels," proclaimed the scholarly schoolmaster. "And my pa's farm is jest a rifle shot up the road. They ain't a running us off neither," Tad was quick to agree. He raised his new Spencer repeating rifle cocked the hammer and squeezed the trigger. "I'd be doggoned if I couldn't hit a fly in the eye with this here shooting iron," declared the resolute red headed lad. The click of that hammer on an empty chamber seemed to sober the four volunteers. They lapsed into silence. Each in their own mind wondering what the next few days would offer. Off in the distance a whippoorwill sounded its nocturnal call.

The next morning an eruption of noise awakened the runaways to military life.

Through sleep fogged eyes they watched Jonathan cinch up his blue tunic and push aside the tent flap. Through the narrow opening they could see Tad tending a boiling pot on a mess fire. They watched the farm boy grease up a frying pan with lard and set it on the grill. The smell of pork fat mixed with the aroma of coffee wafted through the camp site.

Someone nearby was simmering bacon causing their bellies to rumble. All of this was too much for two growing boys. They dressed hurriedly grabbed their mess gear and joined their sidekicks by the fire. Tad was busy sprinkling water on biscuits. He added some pork fat and slipped them in the frying

pan. Jonathan dipped the hard biscuit
in his coffee biting off small chunks
to make it more agreeable. "Gotta get
your own coffee I'll fry you up some
hard tack if you want," murmured the
freckle faced boy as he flipped over
a biscuit. "Ah, yes my friends you
haven't lived until you feasted on
hardtack and coffee for breakfast,"
cracked the mature educator nibbling
away at the food. But the lads were too
hungry to be fussy. They filled their
canteens with hot coffee and let Tad
bounce a hunk of fat soaked biscuit
in their tins. This wasn't the first
time they dined on hardtack. Dinky and
Daniel had prepared that brittle bread
for them in a dozen different ways.
Without hesitation the lads plunged
into their morning meal like it was beef
steak. They had both acquired the coffee habit from the colored boy. Adding
a handful of their sugar rations to a
cupful made the brew even tastier.

Just as the crew finished their morning meal Sergeant Langer approached
carrying a new Spencer. "Get your
rifles und packs und line up in columns
of two's on the road," hollered the
burly sergeant. He continued down the
line of tents ordering each group as

he went. Reaching the last shelter he waited for the final group to assemble. The top kick walked back forming the men into two equal lines. Once again he paced the full length of the more than fifty blue clad recruits physically placing one behind the other. Once he reached the end he looked down between the rows and shouted "forward march." The columns moved clumsily ahead as Sergeant Langer marched in place shouting vun two, vun two as they filed past. He quick stepped up and down the marching men watching their every movement. Vun Two, vun two, again and again he thundered as they continued up the road. Finally he moved to the front of his troopers, but continued to march backwards with the same "vun two, vun two," cadence in staccato like succession. They continued along the heavily traveled path to a firing range. Sixty or more targets were scattered on the hillside. After they reached a row of canopies the top kick shouted "halt." Some of the untrained volunteers thundered into each other, but to their credit sorted themselves out. The sergeant walked the length of the strewn out soldiers checking backpacks, adjusting straps

and showing men how to sling their muskets. Nodding his head in satisfaction
he moved under a canopy to pry open a
cartridge crate. "Spread out along this
line," ordered the top kick, "We are
going to see how goot you can shoot,"
he added. The burly sergeant dropped a
round in each man's hand as he passed.
He handed one to Jonathan and said
"Und now you show me if you can shoot."
The older man held the cartridge in
his hand for a moment uncertain of
how to load the weapon. The Dutchman
took his own rifle inserted a round
in the breech and snapped off a shot
down range. Following instructions
Jonathan pressed a cartridge into his
Spencer took careful aim and fired.
The bullet kicked up dust two yards in
front of his target. "No yank trigger,
yust squeeze em," chided the sergeant.
To demonstrate he placed his finger
over the older man's until the rifle
exploded its missile down range. It
struck right center of the bullseye to
everyone's delight. "Ya, is much better I think," observed the gratified
top kick. He removed the cylinder from
the butt plate of the rifle dropped
seven rounds in the tube placed a single round in the breech and returned

it to Jonathan. "Mit this rifle ve get eight shots. By got ve gif those rebels something to yell about eh grandpa," growled the burly Dutchman. "Well, after watching that demonstration you've certainly convinced me," the school-master replied, still gazing at his new spencer repeating rifle. "Shoot, shoot," the sergeant hollered pointing his finger directly at Jonathan. The mild mannered teacher went obediently to his haunches before sliding into a prone position. He joined a long line of shooters who were becoming accus-tomed to the quick shooting firearm.

Sergeant Langer turned to Tad who seemed to be at ease with the innova-tive weapon. He slipped a cartridge in the boy's hands and said "shoot." The freckle faced lad fired off a round splitting the bullseye dead center. "Goot, goot, ve need men who can shoot by got," exclaimed the Dutchman. He dropped a box of cartridges next to Tad who grabbed them and inserted seven in the receiver tube. He squeezed off six rapid shots. All landed in a neat circle on the right edge of the bull's eye. The top kick grinned, obviously delighted with the farm boy's marks-manship. "Very goot, very goot, let's see you make the otter boy's just as goot," challenged the burly trooper, proceeding to the next group of shooters. By this time the whole line of volunteers were blasting rifle fire down range. The Dutchman stepped back to observe the freckle faced Tad hovering over the runaway's as they rapid fired their weapons. Yep, the lads were learning fast as most youngsters do when they're challenged. But was there enough time to ready this company of green recruits to do battle with veteran southern infantry? They would begin to find that out tonight when the unit moved up as Division Reserves.

The newly formed militiamen broke camp at three o'clock in the morning. They formed on a side road just as the heavens exploded in a series of thunderclaps. Moments later they were engulfed in a heavy downpour. Their new cotton uniforms absorbed water like a sponge, becoming soggy, leaden weights as the deluge continued. A Battalion of artillery sloshed by, there six horse teams kicking up mud to add to the infantrymen's discomfort. Following them a battery of Napoleons trotted up caissons creaking under the

weight of full ammunition chests. The
frail Jonathan wrapped his arms around
a sapling to remain erect. One slip
could cause a man to be mashed like
porridge into the Pennsylvania soil.
"Jest a little ol thunder shower boys.
Gets the rhubarb growing," Tad laughed
with rain cascading from the brim of
his cap. "Some of us just don't travel
the same roads together," lamented the
school teacher.

As the last wagon thundered by captain Daly stepped out onto the road.
Sergeant Langer turned to his troopers
and shouted "Rout Step, March," while
trying to keep his balance on the slippery turf. The line of enlistee's moved
ahead in half steps trying to grip
the wet ground with their feet. Single
freighters swung around them splatter-
ing more wet dirt on their soggy uniforms. Other wagons coming from the
other direction adding to the melee.
"What do you think all this rushing is
about Will?" asked the harried Ambrose
boy. "Doggoned if I know, we couldn't
see them rebs if they were on the other
side of the road," he sputtered wiping
a glob of mud from his lips. "Don't
worry boys it won't be long afore
we bump into a whole passel of them

Johnnies," allowed the farm boy. "I won't be able to do much fighting if they march me much further," groaned the schoolmaster.

CHAPTER SIXTEEN

It was obvious from the beginning that
General Robert E. Lee was inviting the
union forces to a slugging match. He
became convinced his army of northern
Virginia was unbeatable in the field,
either through force of arms or their
ability to out march or out maneuver federal forces. He also realized
the industrial north could overpower
a superior army with its enormous
resources. If his army could win a
convincing victory on Union soil he
could divide the enemy by encouraging
the peace process. If a just ending to
this war for autonomy could not produce better results than a return to
the Union Lee believed the Southern
people would be willing to resume
the war than submit to those terms.
In a letter to Jefferson Davis Lee
stated his belief that powerful ele-
ments in the north would be willing

to concede independence to the south
rather than continue the bloodshed. He
also believed the strength of the Army
of northern Virginia was declining
despite its recent victories. Those
were Lee's convictions as he prepared
for the impending battle.

On the morning of July first in a
hickory grove outside of Cashtown major
general Henry Heth and brigadier general J. Johnstone Pettigrew of the confederate states of America were reading
an article in the Gettysburg Compiler.
"A Mister McPherson has opened a stand
in Centre Square. He has caps and hats
at the lowest of prices. Boots and
shoes including Men's fine calf boots
will be sold at cheap or cheaper prices
than ever," General Heth said reciting
the newspaper advertisement. "We have
read reports of union cavalry between
us and the town," Pettigrew replied.
"We're going after those shoes Jay.
Our men are in dire need of boots as
are many of our officers," declared the
senior commander pointing emphatically
to the paper. "I'll have the brigades
move out," his subordinate responded.
He snapped off an absent minded salute
and left to form his brigades.

The familiar clatter of canteens bouncing against bayonets announced the Southern Forces were entering the road. The column stepped out under clear skies except for an occasional thunder cloud. A long gray line of veteran foot soldiers slogged easily through the Pennsylvania countryside.

From the bell tower of the Lutheran seminary in Gettysburg brigadier general John Buford was scanning the surrounding terrain with his field glasses. Yesterday he had fanned out his nearly three thousand cavalrymen in a five mile radius around the town. His scouts had spotted confederate cavalry only that morning on the northwest perimeter. The union commander was righteously concerned his forces were spread much to thin.

He continued his search peering anxiously through the eyepiece. The officer spotted a cow off in the distance and trained his glasses in that direction. He notices movement behind the animal. Buford refocuses his binoculars on these emerging figures straining to identify them. From the distant tree line spread two rows deep gray clad Infantrymen came into view. From behind a rail fence union soldiers began taking up defensive positions. The general watched the secession- ists scale a wooden barrier continu- ing their advance. Two, three, four, puffs of smoke arose from the union ranks before he hears the tell tale report of Cavalry carbines. Three reb- els drop face first in the meadow as the fascinated brigadier observes the action. Another row of southern troops advances from the trees firing their rifles as they come. Reinforcements scurry about from both sides fall- ing into place behind hurriedly made barricades. Larger groups of butter- nuts infiltrate the tree line prepar- ing to enter the fray. General Buford is visibly shaken by the emergence of these new arrivals. He rushes from his vantage point to the entrance below. The concerned brigadier signals to two mounted troopers who rush to his side. "Take this message to General Reynolds," he shouted to the first man handing him a scribbled note. "Yes Sir," the trooper replied as he gal- loped away. Buford wrote another note, handing it to the second man with the orders "Get this to Meade as fast as you can." The soldier was away in an

instant spurring his mount onward with
quick repetitive kicks.

Union artillery began to enfilade
the Rebel positions. A burst landed in
a clump of trees sending limbs crashing into a group of tethered horses.
The beasts thrash about for a moment,
but moments later dropped heavily to
the earth. One chestnut still kicks,
but is put out of its misery by a shot
from a gray uniformed Johnny. Smoke
drifts across the field mixed with the
smell of gunpowder.

Major general John Reynolds commander of I corps galloped up to General
Buford's side, his horse blasting air
from its lungs. "In what strength are
they John," Reynold's asked, holding
his wide eyed animal in restraint.
"At least three maybe four brigades,"
the Cavalryman replied. The commander
drew a parchment from his glove and
scrawled a message. He handed it to one
of the courier's attached to his command. "Get this to Meade's headquarters," general Reynold's snapped. The
trooper fired off a salute and bounded
off on his mission. "I've told Meade
we'd defend this ground inch by inch,"
declared the senior officer. "We'll be
in need of foot support before long

sir they've got us pretty well outnum-
bered," stated the horse soldier. The
commander signaled the next courier who
rushed to his side. Reynold's scratched
a message on a parchment handed it to
the messenger and shouted "Get this to
Wadsworth." The man saluted and rode
away. "With your permission sir I will
return to my troop," requested the cavalry commander. "I'll ride along with
you General Buford," replied the Senior
Officer. "We're taking heavy musket
fire," the trooper warned. "Thank you
John I realize that, but I need to see
our positions close up so I can determine what we're up against," he persisted. The junior officer grinned in
admiration knowing the General's repu-
tation for getting in the thick of the
fighting. He nudged his mount into a
quick trot with the union commander
gently clicking his sorrel alongside.
Seconds later the two generals were
galloping over a small rise towards
the intense musket fire.

The sounds of this engagement have
alerted the entire countryside. At
Regimental Headquarters of the fourteenth New York Colonel Edward B. Fowler
has been handed a packet by one of general Wadworth's couriers. He tore it

open with his junior officers standing nearby awaiting orders. An air of
electricity enveloped the red legged
troopers for weeks. They have moved
hundreds of miles to a tree ringed
meadow not five miles from Gettysburg.
The Brooklyn regimental colonel rose
from his camp stool to face his anxious unit commanders. "Form your companies on the Emmetsburg road gentlemen
there's rebel Infantry moving down the
Chambersburg Pike. General Wadsworth
wants us to run them off," he said his
voice thundering with conviction. The
junior officers saluted in almost perfect unison; their hands tipping the
ends of their caps as they exited the
tent to return to their troops. An
unmistakable rustling of haversacks
accompanied by the clanging of muskets, of bayonets being hurriedly slung
on belts announced the regiment's muster. Minutes later they wheeled into
position on the well-traveled road.
Captain Andrew Whelan stepped smartly
in front of his veteran troopers. His
Top kick was as usual close to his
side. They were the last company in
the line of march. "I knew when I laid
me eyes on that bloody red sunrise
this very morning we were in for a bit

of a tussle," Gormley remarked, gazing up to the heavens. "They've been marching through our cities as easy as you please, it's time we gave them a fight," said the determined Andrew. He peered up at the plumes of smoke in the distant hills. They had been hearing artillery bursts since morning and these were the tell tale signs.

After a few miles the column moved off the highway abreast of the Lutheran seminary. "Load muskets" was shouted from the front as they formed in line with other New York regiments. The veteran troopers punched rounds in their rifles rammed them home in swift order and pushed on without losing a beat. The red legged Brooklynites formed left of the brigade joining the ninety fifth New York on the portside of the Chambersburg Pike. A railroad cut split between them and three other New York regiments on the right. The sixth Wisconsin marched up on the red legged devils left near a cluster of trees. The entire union line was suddenly struck by a fusillade of rifle fire. Bullets whistled overhead splintering branches as men ducked for cover.

A mile away captain Daly led his
Volunteers across a wide meadow towards
a small rise. Sergeant Langer takes up
the rear to prevent straggling. "Ya,
ya, that's goot boy's, yust a few more
yards," he urged to the sweat drenched
recruits. Tad was first to hit the
crest followed by Bobby and Will.
Jonathan hit the ground three yards
behind them gasping for breath, "Don't
know what all this rushing is about,"
gasped the schoolteacher searching for
air. Artillery shells burst in the
surrounding fields sending dirt cascading in every direction. "Doggone it
Will if the hair on my neck ain't a
fuzzing up," remarked the Ambrose boy.
"Don't you worry none mine's standing
straight out," murmured his partner
trying to bury his face in the turf.
"Yep, mine's straight out too jest like
a cat," exclaimed the freckle faced
lad. "Can't feel a thing myself, but I
darn sure wish I could run," the older
Jonathan confessed.

In the fields below they watched
a thin blue line of union cavalrymen
retreating in an orderly fashion. Men
on foot are firing their carbines into
the advancing Butternuts. Others hold

onto their comrades mounts as they slowly move to the rear. "From back here it looks like they're playing some kind of game," Bobby remarked, viewing the action. Figures were trailing horses and handing the reins to other blue coated men who galloped off to the rear.

The fleeing cavalrymen reached a small hill and hit the ground in a firing position and knocking down a whole line of secessionists. Troopers holding horses moved through their ranks to set up a position behind them in a copse of trees.

Artillery shells fell directly on the union line throwing man and beast into the air. Another barrage exploded over the Federal lines raining metal fragments into the horse soldiers. Only four of the eighteen defenders rose from the smoke to continue their withdrawal. Just as the bluebellies reach the trees gray uniformed figures infiltrate their former positions. They are taken under a brisk fire immediately stopping their advance. Over a dozen secessionists fall in a heap mingling gray with their brethren in blue.

Finally, the fleeing cavalrymen back their way into the New Volunteers

position. Some have been clipped by
secessionist lead, with blood dripping
onto their tunics from facial wounds.
Many have hastily wrapped bandages on
arm wounds; others are helping their
seriously wounded onto wagons. Seeing
this, captain Daly stood up in full
view of the enemy. The inspired officer walked slowly among the conscripts
oblivious to the singing bullets.
"Those rebs are gonna come charging
up that hill and it's up to us to stop
them," he hollered trying to be heard
over the din of battle. By then the
last of the retreating cavalrymen are
safely out of musket range. The secessionist infantrymen moved up the hill
in three waves. The first row leveled their rifles at the militiamen
and fire. When they kneel to reload
the second row moves through them
stopping only to deliver a round of
Minnie balls into the defenders. "Hit
em men," shouted the union officer. He
stood boldly erect with his five shot
Colt Revolver and unloaded it into the
screaming invaders. At that moment his
new Recruits fired a volley into the
front rank knocking half of it to the
dirt. Tad made three shots dropping
a screaming rebel each time. Jonathan

fired slow and deliberate missing with two shots, but felling the third man. Will and Bobby the inseparable friends were almost shoulder to shoulder rapid firing their Spencer's into the charging secessionists.

Three butternuts reached the crest of the hill, but Will drops one man, a bearded three striper wielding a saber. Bobby shot another charging reb ten yards from their position. Four of the blue shirted conscripts bolt from the line and are shot down in the cross fire. The secessionists have driven the surviving Recruits into a semi circle. Captain Daly's uniform is in tatters from Confederate lead, but he gives ground grudgingly. His right ear hung partially down his cheek with blood coursing his shoulder epaulets. Sergeant Langer attempted to bandage the officer's wound, but is knocked down by a bullet to the shoulder. "I'm darn near out of shell's sergeant," exclaimed the company commander.

"Ya, und I haf two" the top kick responded flinging his cartridge box to the ground. Three howling rebel infantrymen rushed headlong at the captain while he's reloading his pistol. Langer stuck his rifle under his

arm and impaled one on his bayonet.
Captain Daly shoots another at close
quarters sending the butternut backwards. The third shoots the union officer at point blank range. The defiant
company commander swung his pistol at
his killer as he crumbled to the turf.
His infuriated top kick rushed the
scessionist smashing him to the ground
with his musket before firing his last
round into the man's lifeless body.
The wounded Dutchman takes his rifle in
one hand swinging it in a wide arc taking down another rebel. Tad blasts two
other southerner's down as they rush
the sergeant. A rebel lieutenant drops
Langer with two shots from a revolver.
Bobby shoots the gray uniformed officer as he's leveling his pistol at the
farm boy. It is all close quarters now
with men clubbing at each other with
rifles. Jonathan stopped a growling
Confederate Corporal with what proves
to be his last bullet. His rifle clicks
when he levels at the next Johnny who
kills the mild mannered school teacher
with a round to the chest. The hill
falls suddenly silent except for the
moaning of the wounded. A squad of
rebel soldiers leveled there rifles
at Tad, Will and Bobby, the remaining

survivors of captain Richard Daly's militia company. A lanky butternut corporal wearing a union officer's hat stepped forward aiming his pistol at the teenagers. "Will you looky here at the young un's who's been a fighting us. The Yankee's must be taking em out a grade school," the corporal exclaimed. "Aint nothing but a passel a pups," agreed a Virginia private. "Get up on yer feet yanks, y'all's gonna be our prisoners," drawled the rebel corporal circling his pistol skyward. With their heads bowed in resignation the boys did exactly as instructed falling in between the gray uniformed veterans who were prodding them with their weapons. They walked single file glancing anxiously at the stretched out bodies of their comrades. A light rain fell for just a moment bringing a welcome breeze to this hot sweltering day. It was no relief to the teenagers now that they were being led towards enemy lines as prisoners.

The fourteenth regiment meanwhile was maneuvering into a skirmish line beyond the Seminary. There is the clang of steel as the entire regiment fixed bayonets. Straightening ranks they move forward at a slow trot.

"Smartly men," Andrew shouted ever conscious of military training. "Ah, but you're a quick stepping lot of red legged devils," quipped sergeant Gormley. Buford's cavalrymen came into view withdrawing in perfect order. One group held the horses while the others poured a steady fire into the pursuing secessionists. Both lines were firing at will with bullets whirring overhead. The red legged troopers of the fourteenth regiment moved up along the entire front to relieve the retiring cavalrymen. "Give them a volley" captain Whelan thundered as his troopers hit the ground.

A fusillade of rifle erupted from the union line shattering the front row of rebels. An artillery barrage landed among the federal soldiers killing six men outright. One dazed bluebelly headed to the rear minus his left arm below the elbow. "Give em another taste of union lead lads," Sergeant Gormley shouted as he leveled his rifle. An instant later the Brooklyn militiamen's line blasted a volley into the charging butternuts stopping it in its place. Another rebel brigade entered the field and fired into the union line causing a break in the ranks. Colonel

Fowler's horse is struck in the head, but the valiant animal remains on his feet. The regimental commander takes a mini ball in the leg, but remains in the saddle. Another withering fusillade erupts from the gray ranks blasting gaping holes hole in the line. Many of the wounded red legs begin retiring to the rear, others fall and will never move again.

A rebel bugler sounds the entrance of still another southern brigade. They rushed forward pouring more lead into the federal forces. The union ranks return fire cutting down half the invading secessionists. Union soldiers fell back on either side, but the fourteenth held its ground. Colonel Fowler observed the southerners advancing on the right and to his rear. He rode to the front of his troopers with bullets whizzing in his ear. "They'll cut us up if we move back. Let's show them Johnnies what we're made of men, charge," he hollered wheeling his mount to the crest of the hill. A loud cheer erupted from the ranks as the red legs came charging out of their positions. They ran straight at the charging butternuts that broke in disorder. The Brooklyn soldiers continued to advance pushing the fleeing Rebels into another federal regiment. General Buford was observing the action when a bullet struck General Reynold's who was standing nearby in the temple killing him instantly. Four troopers from the fourteenth rushed to the fallen union commander and removed him from the field.

The disorganized rebel infantry has been driven into the railroad cut by the fierce assault of the fourteenth. The terrain is much lower giving union troops an advantage. Soldiers from the sixth Wisconsin joined the New Yorkers laying down a withering musket barrage that cuts the exposed southerners down by the dozen. Some of the gray clad infantrymen try to run up the embankment, but are dropped immediately by the union cross fire. "Give it to em lads, we've got the buggers pinched in," sergeant Gormley hollered as he rammed home three balls of buckshot in his musket. "Remember Fredericksburg men," shouted Andrew, his voice thundering across the field. A cheer goes up from the ranks as men chant "remember Fredericksburg, remember Fredericksburg," over and over. "Ay Captain many a fine Brooklyn lad fell on that bloody day," the top kick reflected. The Northern Troopers suddenly eased their rifle fire. They observe the secessionist's running in circles much like rabbits trapped by a pack of coyotes. "Throw down your muskets," boomed a multitude of voices from the union lines. An instant later the dazed southern Infantrymen sling their rifles aside and raise their arms in surrender. Rebel officers move out from the embankment to offer their swords to troopers from the sixth Wisconsin. A stocky union private took hold of confederate general James Archer. He removed the officer's sword and raised it triumphantly overhead. A burst of raucous laughter exploded from the triumphant Northerners. "Now there's a fine sight," captain Whelan remarked with an ever widening grin. "It is that, we've captured the whole bloody brigade," exclaimed the red legged top kick.

The Brooklyn officer could not imagine at the moment he was celebrating victory his younger brother was languishing nearby in a hastily erected Rebel prison. Will was among more than thirty other blue shirted soldiers being held at Downey's tavern in the

town of Gettysburg. The three compatriots sat outside in a fenced yard as
armed sentinel's patrolled the perimeter of the compound. Bobby's left arm
has been bandaged by a local doctor
sympathetic to the confederacy. In the
heat of battle the lad never felt the
bullet crease his forearm. His tunic
hung loosely over his left shoulder.
All of their uniforms show the effects
of the fierce fire fight. There are
numerous small nips in the still bright
blue cotton. But Tad is not ready to
sit the war out as a captive. He's been
watching the outside guards trying to
determine a weakness. "I'm for jumping
that fence once it gets dark," whispered the Farm boy. "That's good with
me long as Bobby's arm is alright,"
Will responded, looking quizzically at
his side kick. "Don't fret about me
none, some of those Johnnies are just
waiting to put a ball in our britches,"
replied the wary Ambrose boy.

A tall weather beaten rebel top sergeant entered the compound. The bedraggled southerner walked slowly amidst
the prisoners gazing into each mans
face as he passed. He looked closely
at the northern prisoners checking
them from head to toe. He stopped long

enough to light a corn cob pipe. The man puffed deeply, the smoke enveloping his face. He stood erect aware every eye was trained on his movements.

Finally, as his face twisted into a sneer he shouted "Get those shoes off bluebellies." A union lieutenant who happened to be the lone officer in the group stepped forward. "I'd like to speak to your commanding officer," he said in a firm demanding voice. "What y'all better do is pull those boots off, that's orders," The six striper sneered in response, puffing away on his corn cob.

A contingent of rebels entered the compound with rifles poised for action. "Okay yanks throw yer boots in a pile or we're gonna come and rip em off your feet," the sergeant roared at his prisoners. Realizing the futility of the situation the union soldiers began removing their shoes.

Shrugging their shoulders in resignation they dropped them into a growing pile. The tattered rebel guards are on the discarded footwear like boll weevils on cotton. While they're scrambling the top sergeant pushes them aside and selects a pair of boots that fits him perfectly. The teenagers know their chances of escape have been narrowed. "Doggoned if we can do much running without shoes," Will was quick to point out. "Yeah, but you gotta give it to them secesh half of them ain't laced on a shoe since they left Dixie," Tad said with grudging admiration.

A confederate colonel entered the compound flanked by two captains and a major. They motioned to the sergeant who rushed to their side. After a short conference the sergeant turned to address the captives. "Simmer down yanks the colonel wants to talk to y'all," he hollered waving his arms to get quiet from the murmuring federals. The rebel commander stepped onto a wooden stool to begin his message. "We're offering you men parole under certain conditions," was his not too convincing opening statement.

The union lieutenant moved to the front of the assembled prisoners. "I want to lodge a protest against your men stealing our shoes," declared the offended northerner. The not very sympathetic colonel looked at his junior officers trying to stifle a laugh. "That's all very good lieutenant, but it won't get them back. Will you consider my terms," asked the southern commander. "It's my duty sir," replied the federal officer. The union troopers moved in closer to hear the banter. "You men will have to sign an oath not to bear arms or in any way aid enemies of the confederacy," the colonel explained. "Those are not the worst terms a man could get," the lieutenant pointed out. A bearded three striped union sergeant stepped forward to disagree. "Don't sound like much of an offer to me," he interjected. "You'll be given safe conduct through our lines. After that you can go home for good," countered the Rebel Leader. "They gotta use men to look after us," cried a voice from the crowd. "That's why they want to cut us loose," another voice joined in. "That's right lieutenant they gotta feed us and guard us just so we can't fight them," added the sergeant. "You men have a choice between Belle Isle or Libby prison or you can head home," the colonel stipulated. "There's something to say for that offer men," said the union officer. "Something they can sit on," growled a Michigan private. "That's right, we wait here our own boys will retake this place," agreed the bearded sergeant. The crowd of blue shirted prisoners murmured in agreement. "We're not accepting your parole," declared the lieutenant to a chorus of cheers from the captives.

With darkness approaching the first day of battle general Robert E, Lee and his aide watched the confederate advance from Seminary hill. Lee trained his field glasses to observe his troops pushing the federal forces from the town. Union soldiers ran through pastures scaling fences along the way.

Some hid in barns or ran into houses to escape pursuing rebel infantry. The union infantry appears to be in complete disarray as they seek the safety of cemetery hill.

"I had not intended to fight here, but we must push the advantage before the whole federal army arrives on this front," Lee murmured absentmindedly. A Courier galloped up the hill and handed a message to the aide. "Word from Stewart he's at Carlisle," exclaimed the junior officer.

"At last, send a message for him to hurry his march," sighed the relieved general. His aide scratched a note on a piece of parchment and handed it to the messenger who galloped off immediately.

On cemetery hill general George Meade
and his aide captain McHugh rode their
mounts to an open area overlooking
Gettysburg. The union commander peered
out over the horizon at the confederate campfires dotting the landscape.
General Winfield S. Hancock rode up to
join the others. "It was one hell of
a fight George. Many brave men fought
and died in those fields," Hancock
declared. "I'm afraid so, but we'll be
meeting up with them again tomorrow,"
the determined Meade replied. "These
are strong natural defensive positions
sir," the junior officer pointed out.
"Well, we might as well fight it here
as anywhere else," was his leader's
view point.

Supply wagons and reinforcements
moved up in bright moonlight all along
the hillside. Artillery pieces can be
heard creaking into position just below
the crest. "What concerns me is much of
the army remains on the roads," Hancock
lamented. "By Morning we'll have ninety
five thousand men up on this front,"
General Meade assured his subordinate.
General Hancock grinned at that bit of
news. "I'm sure General Lee would be
interested in hearing that," he murmured under his breath.

CHAPTER SEVENTEEN

The brilliant maneuvering of the union
forces on that hot humid First day of
July dictated where this critical battle would be fought. Their actions gave
Lee no opportunity to begin the con-
flict on terrain of his own choosing.
The first corps of which the fourteenth
was attached gave a furious account
of themselves during the first hours
of the engagement. A testament to the
ferocity of the battle was their six
thousand killed and wounded including
General Reynolds, the corps commander.

But the red legged evils were themselves in danger of being outflanked
because of that magnificent charge
and subsequent capture of an entire
Mississippi brigade. They received
orders to fall back through Gettysburg
to a new perimeter being formed on
Cemetery Hill. The regiment had been
heavily engaged since early morning,

but they moved out smartly as if on parade.

Despite enemy musket fire from three sides the proud troopers retired in good order. If a man dropped in the ranks another took his place.

As the troops entered the town an exploding artillery shell smashed into a nearby chimney showering Colonel Fowler with brick and mortar. The imperturbable commander set his mount to a slow trot on the cobblestone streets as another shell shattered a stone building wounding two of his soldiers. Confederate canon had found the range of the retreating federals. They poured round after round into the tangled mass of bluecoats trying to extricate themselves from the clogged thoroughfare.

The secessionists were already in possession of the town when union forces began their withdrawal so this was becoming a turkey shoot. Gray uniformed sharpshooters set up in alleyways and fired point blank into the unlucky bluebellies who were withdrawing down the main streets.

Finding it impossible to move in this sea of humanity Colonel Fowler ordered his men to tear down a fence where another alley led to the Emmettsburg Road. With darkness falling the regimental commander maneuvered his troopers to the left rear of the reserve division of the Eleventh Corps who were occupying a strong position behind a stone wall.

All the while his men were engaged with the enemy at close quarters sometimes using muskets to club their way through confederate barricades. Fascinated townspeople peered out through narrow openings to watch men shot on their doorsteps. Some decent souls rushed to assist wounded on both sides. Others hid retreating blue shirts that were separated from their units in cellars or pig barns. Many of these men were later to be taken prisoner by their brothers in gray.

A brisk rain accompanied by a cooling breeze welcomed the troops into their defensive positions near Culp's Hill. The men of the Fourteenth reached into their knapsacks for crumbled hardtack while sipping water from their canteens to make it palatable. They were a grimy lot from the days battle their sweat streaked faces blackened with gunpowder.

But the veteran soldiers knew this battle was far from over.

They began throwing up breastworks to strengthen their perimeter for the next onslaught.

CHAPTER EIGHTEEN

The morning of July 2 opened to overcast skies with a rhythmical like rain pelting the awakening armies. The shouting of sentries and subsequent laughter announced the return of many Blue uniformed stragglers to their units. They had become separated or lost in the town during the previous nights struggle.

Some crawled in sheepishly trying to explain the loss of their muskets and haversacks to grinning compatriots. A few swagger in bearing goblets, souvenirs of a mysterious night in a Gettysburg tavern. Corporal Duffy strolled into Sergeant Gormley's tent brandishing a confederate saber. "And where did you get that pig sticker?" asked the top kick. "I took it off a Rebel Captain," replied the self-satisfied two striper. "Did ye now, well thank you Duffy I've always wanted one to send home to me Dad," exclaimed the Sergeant, removing the blade from his subordinate. The Corporal stood there open mouthed watching the top kick carefully wrap his captured sword in a blanket. When he finished his task Gormley looked over at the befuddled trooper and shouted "Alright Duffy you've been lollygagging around here enough get back to your men." The red faced Corporal opened his mouth, but couldn't seem to speak. He tried again, but the glaring Topkick was just too intimidating a man to argue with over a war trophy. The two striper shrugged his shoulders and left without uttering a word.

During the morning hours small skirmishes erupted along the entrenched federal line. General Meade ordered the fourteenth regiment to be put in reserve, but be prepared to move into any gap that should develop. They posed at the ready as the sounds of a major engagement roared on their left. Union artillery was engaged in a fierce exchange with rebel cannon fire along the vicinity of Round Top.

Later that afternoon the Brooklyn regiment was ordered to move quickly to their extreme right. Andrew led his company along a ridge through thick brush to a spot called Spangler's Spring. As they were forming into line they were taken under fire from the fields below. A line of Butternuts sprang from cover to charge the red legs straight on.

"Looks like those Rebs are spoiling for a fight," declared captain Whelan as he settled in behind the breastworks that were set up by the last federal unit driven from this hill. "There's a passel of them running up just as sweet as ye please," agreed his top kick. He leveled his musket at them just as a volley of artillery crashed amongst the screaming Rebels. The whole line seemed to disappear in the cloud of dust from that mighty blast, but another rebel line formed behind those mangled bodies to resume the assault. A burst of cannon fire fell directly into this new threat leaving a gaping hole in the advance. "Those shells are dropping plumb on their lines," Andrew exclaimed as he watched the rounds explode in an orderly almost perfect row.

Through the rising cloud of smoke and dust a ragged bunch of undeterred Confederate Soldiers plodded upward towards the entrenched Fourteenth. "Hit them men," shouted Sergeant Gormley as he squeezed off a round hitting a hatless butternut. A fusillade of musket fire erupted from the red legged troopers cutting the gray line in pieces. Rebel cannon suddenly exploded over the northern lines sending hickory trees crashing amongst the defenders. Pieces of the union barricade go tumbling down the hill creating a huge breach in the line. The southern infantry rushed towards this opening with renewed vigor. Andrew jumped from his position to pull two wounded troopers from the maze of lumber and earthworks. His top kick dropped a howling secessionist as he mounted the blockade. "Keep a steady fire on em, men," Gormley hollered as he rammed a ball down his musket. His troopers responded with a volley of rifle fire cutting down the first line of gray clad soldiers. The rebels fired back sending a volley of mini balls whirring into the federal ranks. The Union color bearer was torn apart by lead fragments. He stood frozen for a moment still trying to urge his comrades on when another flurry of lead smashed him to the dirt. Just as his shattered staff fell across his body another red legged trooper scooped it in his hands and raised it above his head. "C'mon, ye bloody devils we've got some hot union lead for ye," hollered the roused top kick as he bounded over the barricade. He rushed at a surprised butternut Lieutenant sinking his bayonet deep into the man's rib cage.

Andrew scaled the abutment to join his enraged Sergeant on the hillside. Gormley meanwhile was pursuing two secessionists who threw down their rifles when the wild eyed Irishman pinned them against a tree with his musket.

"Get them blackards to the rear," the top kick hollered to a nearby trooper who took the relieved Southerners in tow. A resounding cheer rose from the union lines when the battered butternut line broke and ran. Red legged troopers moved atop their ramparts to fire a volley into the retreating rebels. Captain Whelan rushed to the front of his command holding his pistol aloft. "Let's get after them men we've got them on the run," he shouted, his voice roaring with intensity. The red legged New Yorkers came charging out of their pits with a holler, stopping to fire a fusillade of lead into the withdrawing Secessionists. A Rebel sergeant tending a leg wound sat calmly on a stump firing his pistol like a man taking target practice. He dropped two of the charging Yankees before A Brooklyn stevedore put a ball in his chest.

It was almost a complete rout with the confederates fleeing in disorder. One group of rebels held their ground around a

tall young Lieutenant. They dropped four of Captain Whelan's men before the red legs were upon them. A butternut lunged at Gormley with a bayonet, but Andrew blasted him at point blank range. The stubborn secessionists grappled at close quarters not giving an inch. A wild round caught the confederate officer in the forehead, killing him instantly. Gormley clubbed another butternut to the ground with his musket. The remaining rebels raised their hands seeming to lose heart at the loss of their leader. "Get the beggars up that hill" shouted the top kick to his victorious troopers. As the prisoners were led away Andrew watched the southern forces withdraw across the fields below. Off in the distance the roar of cannons indicated another skirmish being fought. "We've whipped them this time for fair and good Captain," Sergeant Gormley exclaimed. "Lee's not finished yet he's tried the right and now I suppose he's hitting the left," Andrew replied as he peered off into the distant hills.

"Ay, but the lad's have taken the measure of those howling Butternuts. If they move on our front we'll give em more of the same," said the confident Topkick. Captain Whelan seemed deep in thought as he watched the artillery barrage fall on the Union left. Moments later with darkness creeping over the fields Federal Cannon responded by pounding Confederate positions.

The people of Gettysburg huddled in their homes as the battle raged around them, but many of the local pubs did a brisk business with the thirsty Secessionists. One rural farmer did especially well selling jugs of moonshine to the Southern boys who seemed to prefer Corn liquor. Downey's Tavern where the Teenagers were being held was closed to regular business. He made quite a profit by selling spirits from his side door. The wary proprietor wouldn't accept Confederate money so many a Rebel Officer slipped inside the narrow portal to pay in Union greenbacks.

In the wide compound at the rear of the Pub the irrepressible Tad was not a contented prisoner. Nor were the runaways satisfied to remain behind those dismal fences.

All day they had heard the thump, thump, of artillery shells drum beating the countryside.

As darkness began to settle in the Farm Boy grew even more restless. He stood near the fence watching a Confederate Sergeant lead off two of the three sentries who usually patrolled the outside perimeter. "I'll be doggoned if they ain't daring us to hightail it out of here. They just cut the guards from three to one," murmured the Freckle Faced lad. "That how you reckon it Will," whispered the Ambrose boy. "It might just be so. With all that fighting going on we're just a bother to the Johnnies," young Whelan was quick to assure them. The boys watched the lone guard come into view at the far end of the compound. He was an older man who puffed constantly on a corn cob pipe. Since yesterday they had observed this elder Secessionist Soldier amble his way

around the compound. They had pretty
much timed his movements because of his
slow deliberate pace. "Once he turns
that corner we gotta get up and ske-
daddle over that fence," declared the
Farm Boy. Will looked intently at his
sidekick and said "Remember, the three
of us gotta hit that fence together."
To which Bobby nodded his head in agreement. The Butternut proceeded along
his route twice cupping his hands to
re-light the pipe. When he reached the
far end of the complex he stopped to
tap the ashes from his corn cob. Tad
was watching the man's every movement.
"That doggoned Reb ain't ever gonna
get that corner turned," the exasperated Farm Boy exclaimed. An instant
later the man was gone. "That's it,"
murmured Tad as he bolted towards the
fence. Just as planned they hit the
top section of wood simultaneously.
The lads vaulted over the structure
as one, landing in loose gravel on
the other side. To their credit not
one howl escaped from the youngsters,
but they did begin to run up on their
toes. Tad turned into an alleyway with
the runaways on his tail. "Gosh darn
it Tad how is it you always know which
way to go?" Bobby asked as he pulled up

alongside the Farm Boy. "My Dad use to
have a market here," Tad replied. The
freckle faced youngster looked around
to get his bearings before heading off
again. Seconds later they were on a
cobblestone street that made the going
easier. Their feet slapped on the hard
surface made slippery by a light driz-
zle. Reaching the end of the street Tad
stopped again to familiarize himself
with the surroundings. Satisfied, he
started towards an open meadow. "This
way," Tad whispered "we'll go South up
Stevens run," he added. But a volley
of musket fire from behind a stone wall
drove them to the ground. More rifle
shots rang out causing them to seek
shelter behind a shed. They're on all
fours now crawling as fast as they can
back to the clearing. Tad began to run
with the Runaways just behind in single
file. The Farm Boy led his pack off to
the left skirting McMillan woods on the
right. Another fusillade of fire from
the tree line drove them to a group
of houses. Bullets smacking against
the stone wall forced them into a two
story house. Once inside they noticed
a flickering candle light coming from
an adjoining room. Will motioned to
the others to enter one door while he

takes the other. The daring Tad rushes headfirst through the doorway. All three are surprised to see a wounded Union Private lying next to a wounded Rebel Corporal. Both are bleeding from apparent musket wounds. "You got any water," mumbled the Federal Soldier. "We don't have a drop," Will replied. "Sure could use a drink, there's a barrel in that other room," stated the wounded Yankee. Bobby went to the next room and returned with a tin of water. He handed it to the Blue Uniformed soldier who quickly guzzled it down. The Rebel Corporal raised himself up on his elbows as if trying to speak. Suddenly, the man slipped backwards gasping for breath the blood oozing from his lips. An instant later he rolled over dead. "That Johnny drug me here from Culp's hill, said I was his prisoner," murmured the bleeding Private. "He jest up and died," declared the Farm Boy. "His own kind shot him up the road a ways. I dragged him in here," said the Union Private. "How bad are you hurt," queried the Ambrose boy. "I'm gut shot, I ain't gonna make it for sure," the wounded man declared. "You can't say that for sure maybe we can find a doctor," Bobby replied, while looking anxiously for his friends to concur. "Nah, they can't help with this," the Private acknowledged with a weak shrug. The man opened his shirt to display a gaping stomach wound. He raised the tin cup to his lips and helped himself to a deep drink. "Better go easy on that water," cautioned the Whelan boy. "I'd be obliged if you'd mail this letter to my Ma and Pa," The Soldier asked handing Bobby a soiled envelope. Once again he tried to sip from the cup, but fell back with his eyes fixed on the ceiling. "Gosh darn war," shouted the angry Ambrose lad. "Ain't nothing fair Bobby not nothing at all," Will uttered with a deep sigh "Least ways two of us got shoes," the Freckle Faced Farm Boy commented.

Meanwhile at Robert E. Lee's Headquarters on Seminary Ridge the General is startled from his map reading by the appearance of his Cavalry Commander General Jeb Stuart. "Ah, I see you've finally arrived," announced the Southern Commander. "My apologies sir, but we did engage the enemy," the Horse Soldier replied in his own defense. "General, your cavalry is the eyes and ears of this army yet I have received no word from you on the disposition of federal Forces," was Lee's chiding response. "I will resign if my error in judgment has caused you difficulty," replied the fiercely loyal Stuart. "No Jeb, all I ask is that you help me fight these people," confided the Rebel leader. The two Southern Generals looked at each other for a moment with a deep respect reserved for comrades in battle. Not another word was exchanged but Stuart felt blistered by the reprimand.

CHAPTER NINETEEN

On July 3 just as daylight began streaking the Pennsylvania countryside a cannonading erupted on the Union right. Once again General Lee was trying to pry open the Union fish hook. During the night two of his Regiments gained some ground on Culp's Hill, but a deadly fire from entrenched Federal forces drove the Rebels back to their lines.

At Union Headquarters on Cemetery Hill General Meade was at that moment perusing his maps when General Hancock entered to file his report. "It appears our lines are complete General," the Junior Officer declared. "I would not advise one of my commanders to move his positions on this day," stated the Union leader. "You've no doubt heard General Sickles has given his leg to the Union," Hancock replied with the hint of a grin coursing his face. "Yes, but Daniel's a politician it will bode him well in Tammany Hall I suppose," the dour Commander pointed out. "On this day it will bode well if we knew where General Lee will attack us next," quipped the subordinate. The Union Commander sauntered over to his chart board to point a finger at a circle drawn on the map. "Right here General Hancock," Meade emphasized, his voice brimming with conviction. "You expect him to strike your center?" exclaimed the puzzled Hancock. "He has struck our right, he has tried out left. Every Private in our army expects him to hit our center," explained the Union Commander.

In the village below the teenagers were peering out the second story windows at the exploding artillery. "Ain't no sense us trying to get back through that cannon fire," declared the Whelan Boy. "Maybe if we just sit here our own boys might come walking right on by," was Tad's not to convincing reply. "Doggoned if I know where our Regiment is," Bobby said in his usual candid manner. "Not much of the One Hundred sixteenth Pennsylvania left cepting us," declared the Farm Boy. "I'd sure like to know where my brother Andrew is. I know the Fourteenth is out there somewhere," Will Said peering towards the Union positions.

At the very center of the Union lines Colonel Patrick Kelly of the Irish Brigade stood with William Corby the Brigade Chaplain. Artillery shells landed in the fields nearby showering them with debris. Soldiers were scurrying about throwing aside their eating utensils and grabbing their rifles. "I'd like to offer a general absolution for the men if you could spare a moment," offered the fiery Man of the Cloth. "I'd say it was a fine time to cleanse a man of his sin," replied the Union Officer. The Colonel waved to a subordinate who shouted "Order Arms" the men positioned their muskets at order arms as the Parson mounted a huge flat boulder. The Man of God extended his arms to the heavens in supplication as he began to speak. "Men of the Union, yours is a sacred trust. You fight for what is noble in the sight of God. You must remember my sons Holy Mother Church refuses Christian burial to those who turns their back on his foe. If you would kneel I will grant absolution to each of you who makes a sincere act of contrition," he said,

his voice booming over the countryside. There was a clanging of rifles
as the men kneel. A loud murmur erupted
from the crowd of Union Soldiers as
they completed their prayer. The men
returned to their feet to the order
"Form your companies." The Chaplain
remained in his exposed position on
the rock while the column proceeded
to their entrenchments. Seconds later
the entire area is put under bombardment by Confederate Cannon. Hundreds
of shells begin falling at the center
of the Union line.

On Cemetery Hill two shells land
outside Union Headquarters sending
General Meade rushing outside. Another
shell lands at the rear of the building
causing much of it to collapse. Captain
McHugh rushed to assist the Commanding
officer who is brushing dust from
his uniform. "Are you alright sir,"
asked the Aide, he too, shaken by the
blast. "Just a bit dusty" cracked the
Commanding Officer. A shell landed on
a nearby wagon throwing its occupants
to the ground. Three men are killed
outright and four more are seriously
wounded. Two horses lay dead amongst
their traces. "They've got us brack-
eted" shouted the Union Captain. "I'd

say it's time to move Headquarters,"
Meade replied as more shells crashed
into the tree tops. "Yes Sir, I'll get
the horses," hollered the Aide racing
to the tethered animals. A few seconds
later they galloped away.

From their second story vantage
point the boys observed the initial
Rebel barrage land on Federal Lines.
The entire hillside was ringed with
explosions. A group of shells liter-
ally splintered a wooden barricade.
Blue uniformed bodies lay strewn in the
wreckage. Fifteen or more horses were
scattered about the ruins. A direct
hit on an artillery caisson shakes
their small house to its foundations.
Suddenly the Union artillery begins
its response. Shells begin falling in
the fields slowly walking their way to
the tree line.

Amongst this fierce cannonade the
boys watched the Confederate Officers
on horseback trying to steady their
men. They ride among the ranks stopping to talk with troopers along the
way. One brave Butternut moves out
into the open to gallop his steed
along the entire front. A loud
cheer erupted from the ranks of the
Secessionists.

A Rebel band sounds Dixie as the Southern army emerged from the trees. They dressed ranks in perfect order as if forming for a review. "God, if that ain't the scariest thing I ever saw," Bobby exclaimed as he viewed the assembling Rebels. "Yes sir, I'm sort of glad now we're in this house," declared the fascinated Will. Tad was readying a rifle he found next to the dead Rebel Corporal. "That Reb had his self a fine musket," said the Freckle faced Farm Boy. He moved to the window as the Confederates marched across the field. "Doggoned if they ain't aiming to hit our lines straight on," Tad declared in unconcealed admiration. "Looks like the whole Reb army's coming out of them woods," cried the Whelan boy. A fusillade of Federal Cannon crashed into the Butternuts sending bodies flying through the air.

"No man can cross those fields and live," was Bobby's awed comment. "They're still a coming," Tad was quick to point out. "Just like they're on parade," Will observed.

The Grey Uniformed wave of humanity continued its inexorable march towards a distant copse of trees. Exploding artillery cut through their ranks smashing the brave soldiers to the ground. "Those Johnnies got more backbone than sense," was Tad's grudging comment.

Bobby gasped as he observed the Rebel line falter for a moment, but once again they dressed ranks to press onward.

A Butternut Officer turned to reassure his troops when a round of solid shot just cut him in half. The veteran infantrymen moved up to fill the ranks as their comrade's fell. "Doggoned if I don't hate that gray uniform, but I can't hate a man when he's being blowed apart," exclaimed the compassionate Ambrose boy.

The Southern line disappeared into a depression startling the onlookers, but moments later they came into view. Three shells strike one section of the reappearing line four rounds blast another sending dozens of men crashing to the turf. From the tree line forward a trail of gray uniforms follow the Confederate advance. "A musket ball doesn't care who it hits or what color a man's wearing," sighed the Farm Boy as the Gray line moved closer to Federal lines. The cannoneers loaded buckshot into their muzzles. They lowered their

pieces to fire point blank into their
enemy. Entire sections of the Butternut
advance faded away.

At a hundred yards the Union infantry raised up out of their pits to
unload screaming bits of lead into the
Rebels.

Almost the entire Confederate front
fell in a hail of bullets. Another group
of Butternuts fill in only to be slaugh-
tered by rifle fire. The Gray line
reached the stone wall and was blasted
back as they attempted to climb over.
One saber wielding Rebel officer mounted
a Federal Cannon, but as he turned to
rally his troops he's shot down.

Federal troops are falling in their
entrenchments from the attacking
Butternuts. A mounted Union officer
is shot from his horse as he charges
headlong into the enemy. Union troops
rush from behind their barricades to
fight at close quarters. A Rebel colonel is shot in the melee. A Confederate
Sergeant clubs a Union Captain to
the ground with his musket. A Union
Corporal impales a charging Butternut
on his bayonet. Smoke begins to drift
eerily across the embattled enemies.
Much of the fighting is concentrated
near the clump of trees.

John Jack McGuire

Groups of Confederate wounded stream back across the field. Realizing they're cut off other Rebels climb back over the fences to begin their retreat. Union troopers from the left and right move from there pits to blast away at the withdrawing enemy. Men on both sides are falling from the disorganized Musket fire. Fleeing secessionists carry wounded comrades as they fall back. Union troopers begin to chant "Fredericksburg, Fredericksburg, at the retreating Butternut infantrymen. "They're moving back, they're beat, we've got em on the run," shouted the Whelan Boy. "Ain't that the purtiest sight you ever did see," Tad declared. "It's over, thank God, that's what I care about," said the relieved Ambrose lad.

Groups of Rebel stragglers came into view returning slowly to their lines. Some are helping wounded comrades others appear to be in a state of confusion. They stumble around as if shell shocked from the cannonading. Tad raised his musket to take a Butternut corporal in his sights. "Leave him be," shouted Bobby knocking the rifle from the Farm Boy's hands. "That's the enemy Bob," proclaimed the chastened Tad. "There's been enough killing today," asserted the Ambrose Boy.

The battlefield appears almost silent, but for an occasional musket blast. Union soldiers moved out of their barricades in large numbers to celebrate this victory. Some gather up rifles while others help wounded Butternuts. Federal stretcher bearers began tending the more seriously injured.

As the last bunch of Southern stragglers was fading into the tree line the teenagers made their way out of the house. The boys walked slowly peering across the open meadow at Gray clad Southerners oozing their life's blood into the Pennsylvania soil. Off to their right a dazed Rebel staggered to his feet still grasping his musket. He stumbled about for a moment before dropping back to his knees. The lads watched in fascination as the confused soldier raised the rifle to his shoulder. Suddenly the weapon exploded sending a mini ball smashing into Tad's chest. The Farm Boy forced a sickly grin as he slumped to the ground. "No, doggone it no, you ain't hit bad are you Tad," cried the Ambrose boy. Tad tried to speak, but only a streak of blood oozed from his lips. Again, he tried to smile, but the color drained from his Freckled Face. His eyes fixed on his friends for just a moment before he drew his last breath. Bobby grabbed his comrades rifle took careful aim and fired a round into his murderer killing him instantly. The enraged Ambrose boy took the musket and smashed it on the ground splintering it into pieces. He grabbed the Butternut's rifle breaking it in half with one swing. "I don't ever want to shoot a man again not ever," he screamed, his voice quaking with emotion. The grieving teenager knelt down next to his stricken friend to tidy up his tunic. "Doggone it Tad I wish I could tell you how sorry we are, you were the bravest of the brave," he murmured as he snapped the last button closed. "Doggoned if he wasn't" sobbed his sidekick. Will ambled off a short distance surveying the human wreckage strewn about in the most grotesque positions. "I reckon it's hard for anyone to make sense of this," he said gazing at four crumpled Southern Soldiers who died together fighting for their cause. He walked back to his sidekick to pay his last respect to the fallen Tad. Bobby was whittling away on a piece of wood he had broken off a Confederate ammunition crate. He placed the tablet on his Friend's chest and attached it to his tunic with a shoelace. It read "Tad Collins, 116th Pennsylvania, a Farm Boy who died for the Union."

Andrew was thumbing through the casualty list handed to him by Sergeant Gormley. "We've got near ninety listed as missing sir," the Topkick declared. The Trooper turned around waiting for an answer, but the Captain was looking open mouthed at the figure standing in the tent flap.

"Seeing as we're related Colonel Fowler said we could come visit," young Whelan said as he stepped inside. "Will, is that you, is that really you standing there," exclaimed the incredulous Officer. Trying to remain as military as possible Will rushed forward to embrace his older brother. "We were looking for the Regiment but never could find you. Then we joined up with the Pennsylvania Militia," the younger boy professed. "You fought here at Gettysburg," shouted the surprised Union Captain as he checked his kid brother over for wounds. "Well, sort of, until we got captured," the boy replied in a hushed voice. Andrew had to stifle a laugh as he looked at his younger brother standing there in his Blue Uniform. "Here I am thinking you're safe back there in Brooklyn and you're over the next hill getting yourself shot at" the elder Whelan maintained. "We just had to get away from Mister Gingrich. He'd have whipped us good by now," Will said trying to defend his actions. "Well, I can tell you something about Gingrich. He was caught selling food that was meant for the kids in the home. Yep, I heard they put him in jail for three years," Andrew stated. He displayed a news article from the Brooklyn Eagle and showed it to the runaways "You hear that Bob old Whip Gingrich's been put in jail for stealing," exclaimed the Whelan boy. "I'm hoping he gets a taste of that leather he's been laying on everyone else," exclaimed the Ambrose boy.

Sergeant Gormley stepped out of the tent and returned with a pitcher of milk and a tray of peach cobbler. "Here ye go lads ye must be dry after all that talking," grinned the Irishman. He tipped his hat to the lads and made his exit into the gathering darkness.

While the boys munched on their treats punctuated by large gulps of milk Andrew left for Regimental Headquarters. He met with Colonel Fowler to discuss his younger brother's militia involvement. Captain Whelan explained how the underage boys stretched the truth to enlist in the Militia.

The Brooklyn Commander assured him he would dispatch an Adjutant to Union Headquarters to bring this matter to a happy conclusion. Andrew thanked the Commanding Officer and returned to his tent. The lads were huddled in a corner asleep as were most of the soldiers in the campsite. He settled into his camp chair to join the boys in slumber.

At first light a courier entered the shelter to place a packet on Andrew's field table. After the soldier left the Captain read through the papers with great interest.

Sergeant Gormley entered carrying a slab of ham mixed with a platter of eggs. He placed it on the table with a pot of coffee. The smell of food appeared to roust the lads from their resting place. "C'mon me buckoes if ye want some of this fine grub," chortled the Topkick. They rushed to the table as the Trooper ladled the food on separate platters.

The Runaways ate like men condemned to the gallows, much to the amusement of Will's elder brother. He was also amazed at the amount of coffee they drank. Captain Whelan drew one of the papers from the packet and began to read. "Private Robert Ambrose will immediately proceed to Philadelphia by Military freighter where he will be discharged from the Pennsylvania Militia effective upon arrival signed General George Meade Commanding General, Army of the Potomac," he said, reading quickly from the text. "How did that happen," the ecstatic Bobby exclaimed. "You've got a friend in the right places," Andrew replied with a gesture of his hand. "I'm happy for you Bob I know it's what you wanted," the Whelan boy interjected. "Yes, and there's one here for you that reads exactly the same way little brother," said the Captain with a wide grin. "Doggone it Andrew you're always surprising me like that," shouted Will rushing to his brother's side. "You're going back to school. Major Jordan has made arrangements for you and Bobby to attend the Delehanty Boarding School in Brooklyn. You'll be working there as apprentice gardeners until the new semester begins." The Captain said handing his brother an official looking parchment. "Thank you Captain Whelan I will always be obliged," said the grateful Ambrose Lad. "You know Andrew I don't think we'll mind going back to school," admitted the chastened Will.

A large Chestnut Colt pulling a surrey stepped in front of the tent. "Okay boys, you're on your way," said the Captain motioning to the cart. "Already," shouted the boys in unison. "Yep, no time to change your minds" grinned the Union Captain. Bobby shook the officer's hand as did his younger brother in an attempt to appear more mature. All three exchanged snappy salutes before the lads bolted to the carriage. They hopped aboard the cart waving to Andrew as the horse turned onto the roadway. The animal trotted briskly on the circular path whizzing by the many Regiments encamped on the hillside. A quarter of a mile down the lane they noticed a long line of Bluebellies awaiting their turn for the Johnny Cakes being ladled out by Dinky Dolan.

Daniel stood nearby sporting a Dress Blue Army uniform.

"You see that Will, old Dinky Dolan's back in business and Daniel's all decked out in Army Blue," Bobby exclaimed.

"Yep, I wonder what he's asking for those Johnny Cakes," Will laughed.

12708961R00129

Made in the USA
Charleston, SC
22 May 2012